THE
LEGEND
OF THE GREEN
WOLF RIDER

Ethan,

GDHoward

For Toffee

*My gentle companion as we walked in the
fields and the woods whilst marvelling at all
nature's wonders ... especially the deer*

Crumps Barn Studio
No.2 The Waterloo, Cirencester GL7 2PZ
www.crumpsbarnstudio.co.uk

Text and illustrations copyright © G. D. Howard 2023

Cover design by Lorna Gray

Printed in the UK by Severn, Gloucester on responsibly sourced paper

ISBN 978-1-915067-33-3

THE LEGEND OF THE GREEN WOLF RIDER

G.D. HOWARD

Crumps Barn Studio

PART 1

OUT OF THE DARK

1

DIFFERENT LIVES

O N A MOONLIT night, a cool summer wind blows steadily through a vast wild forest. From the murky distance, a solitary owl hoots, its shrill call echoing through the silent woodland.

Slowly the dark line of the treetops against the streaked sky reveals a silhouette of a forbidding castle. This is a large construction of stone and timber set within a huge, blackened clearing – a clearing devoid of vegetation of any sort, other than tree stumps and rough tufts of dying grass.

A strong wooden outer wall protects the two depressing buildings within its perimeter – the only entrance and exit is through a wooden doorway that houses two heavy wooden gates, now firmly locked. The ominous castle does not look like a place of light, warmth and laughter.

It all looks deserted except for the plumes of grey wood smoke that rise lazily into the night sky from two chimneys, and the glow of a flickering light from a lone window set high within the stone tower.

That light belongs to a fire in a great hall. A large man sits alone on a throne-like seat by the blazing hearth. He is scowling and deep in thought. His matted hair falls either side of his bearded face and onto his sleeveless leather tunic where two muscular bare arms, with large hands, rest on his ample stomach. The arms and hands look dark with hair but, taking a closer look you would have seen that the dark colouration was not hair but a network of black veins. These same dark veins can also be seen on his neck and his face where his beard doesn't grow.

He looks, and is, a cruel man. In the past he was an honest and good warlord, but times have changed so now he lives deep in the forest with hunting and killing his only pleasures. The stone walls of the hall are covered in mounted trophies of the animals he has destroyed – the heads of deer, bears, wolves, wild boar and the ferocious forest bull-like aurochs.

In another oppressive room with a cooking fire and a long wooden table, twenty hooded men are eating their evening meal – outcasts from the world they have harmed, who have now found sanctuary in the castle, offering their services to the cruel warlord in return for food and shelter.

One of the men rises and, picking up a carcass of freshly killed meat from the cold stone floor, he heads outside to a wooden enclosure where a pack of eight slavering hunting dogs howl and bark with anticipation of the food to come. He carelessly tosses the carcass to the pack and they fall upon it, growling savagely, tearing it to bits. As the man turns to return to his meal he pauses and looks up. As he does, the moon overhead goes behind a cloud, almost as if it can't bear to watch the scene below.

MANY MILES TO the south of the castle, the moonlight shines down on a small village of low wood and thatched cottages. Warm lights glow from the many small windows and plumes of smoke curl into the night sky from the stone chimneys that protrude from the thatch. There is the comforting sound of the noisy clamour of family life. Peering through the window of one of the houses at the centre of the village you would see a family sitting around a rough wooden table in front of a fire, sharing a simple but nourishing supper of soup and bread. They are talking excitedly to one another and laughing out loud. In another house, there is a similar homely scene with happy people all sitting together eating their supper. The village, washed by the moonlight, is a jumble of rough cottages, a welcoming place and one of warmth, light and cheerfulness.

Set apart a short distance from the main cluster of the village dwellings, is a small cottage. It sits closer to the edge of the forest, where a husband and his wife with their young daughter, Holly, are sitting in front of the warm fire telling stories after supper. Boda, the mother, is talking in hushed tones about a legend from long ago when brave, good warriors who died in battle against evil forces that threatened the woodlands, were buried deep in the forest they had saved, in a special underground chamber, known as a barrow.

Holly giggles and says, 'A burrow?'

Both parents laugh. 'No, a barrow, burrows are where rabbits live!'

'I've seen lots of rabbit burrows,' says Holly, smiling, 'but I've no idea if I've ever seen a barrow.'

'Probably not,' agrees her father Eryk. 'They are supposed to be here in the forest, as the legend says, but even with all my years in the forest, I have never knowingly come across one before.'

'Are they scary places?' asks Holly quietly.

'No, I don't think so.' Her mother pats her hand reassuringly. 'They are places of peace and quiet, somewhere that would attract the animals and birds of the woodlands.'

Leaning forward, Eryk speaks in a quiet and hushed voice. 'I also have a mysterious story for you, Holly – again about a forest legend.'

'Oh, please tell, please tell,' Holly cries excitedly, whilst his wife looks at him with a warning raised eyebrow, as if to say not to scare their daughter just before bedtime.

Smiling and taking a deep breath, her husband begins, 'The legend I am talking about – which was told to me by young Edmund one of the forest foragers, and he said his father told him – is this. That whenever these forests and woodlands are threatened, and evil stalks within the trees, a green figure will arise from within the depths of the forest and ride to fight whatever that evil threat is.'

He pauses for effect, then looking his daughter

straight in the eyes he adds, 'on the back of a huge grey wolf!'

'Oh wow – is that really true – has it happened – have you seen it?' questions a very excited Holly in one breath.

'No, it's not necessarily true,' interrupts her mother, 'it's a legend – we don't know if it has happened or ever will, and no matter what your father might tell you, I can assure you that neither he, nor Edmund, has ever seen any green figure riding on a grey wolf, or any other large beast of the forest for that matter!'

Soon afterwards both parents remind her it's time for bed and they say goodnight to their sleepy daughter. After goodnight kisses, Holly climbs a rickety wooden ladder to her tiny bedroom under the rafters and, before settling down she looks out of the small open window to gaze up at the full moon moving high above the clouds. It seems to be looking down on her. Snuggled up in her warm bed, her dreams that night are not of riding a huge grey wolf but of a secret, sunny place in the forest where rabbits and deer play on a grassy mound full of meadow flowers, birds sing, and all is at peace. It is a lovely, restful dream.

2

KIND DEEDS AND
AN IDEA

THE EARLY SUN was streaming in a bright golden beam through the small window into Holly's room. The bedroom was small with just enough space for Holly's bed, a wooden stool and several wooden pegs for Holly to hang her few clothes on. The window had been cut into the wooden wall, and as it was just an opening, a piece of cloth was kept nearby that could be hung across it to keep the wind and rain out if needed.

The sunbeam shining through the window woke Holly, who stretched, got out of bed, dressed and climbed down the ladder to greet her parents, who were already eating the morning meal. They had to be up early since Holly's father worked as a forester and his contribution to village life was to provide wood for making or repairing houses, and growing and planting new tree saplings in parts of the forest he and his fellow foresters had cleared. He also provided smaller pieces of wood so that the villagers could make whatever furniture they needed for their homes or for use in the small fields they tended on the edge of the village. Finally, as no piece of wood was ever wasted, he and the other foresters also provided firewood for the many village fires.

Holly's mother also had busy days since she too worked in the forest. She worked alongside her husband on the lighter forestry work, and also gathered berries and roots, or grew special plants and flowers in their garden that were good to eat. She was also very skilled at baking oat cakes and simple bread loaves on the hot stones that stood around the front of the fire, making flower or berry cordials from produce she gathered when the season was right (Holly's favourite was elderflower cordial), and mixing her special medicines from ingredients she found in the woods or grew in her garden. These medicines were so effective Holly's mother was often asked by other villagers if she had something to make an upset tummy go away or a headache disappear, and sometimes a special warm poultice to apply to a cut so as to keep it clean and help it heal more quickly.

Holly had just two jobs and they were to sweep the house floors and the garden paths to keep them clean and free of dust, leaves and anything else that shouldn't have been on them.

Holly raced through her breakfast and her jobs and then headed off to her favourite place – the forest that surrounded her house and the village.

She loved walking among the many trees and bushes trying to see the animals that lived there. Her only regret was that she didn't have a pet scampering loyally by her side. Stepping quietly between the tall trees and around the many bushes growing below them, Holly kept her eyes and ears open for a sound or glimpse of colour or movement that would tell her one of the forest creatures was nearby.

Not only did Holly not have a pet, she also had no friends in the village of her own age. When Holly had been about one year old a terrible disease came to the village causing the small children to fall seriously ill. Only Holly survived this disease, but it meant she had no companions of her age to play with. She was sometimes very lonely. That was the reason she had made the forest her friend and all the creatures that lived in it, she just wished the forest creatures saw her as someone to be trusted and not run away when she approached.

Holly was walking alongside a small stream as it wended its way through oaks, elder, beech and pine trees. The water babbled and bubbled as it flowed over black moss-covered rocks. Little fish darted in the shallows, and the bright blue flash of a kingfisher caught Holly's attention as it dived into the water to chase the fish. Smiling she made her way through the warm, green forest until she came to a sun-dappled clearing, in the middle of which stood a gaunt ancient oak tree, once hit by lightning in a storm many years past.

The lightning bolt had partially split the wide trunk. Although the tree had died after that storm damage long ago it still offered shelter to some birds and small animals. Rabbits had made their homes in a series of burrows in the tree roots, and a tawny owl had its home in a large hole high up in the upper trunk.

However, Holly's favourite creature was the green woodpecker that had made a home in one of the many holes in the lower trunk of the tree, just above the place where the tree had split. She loved to see the green and red flash of colour as the bird flew quickly to its nesting hole on returning from gathering food amongst the leaves, pine needles and cones on the forest floor.

As she slowly approached the tree, she saw something that made her stop mid-step. The grasses below the trunk of the tree were moving frantically, and one of the woodpeckers was letting out a piercing distress call. *What on earth could be upsetting them like that,* she thought.

With small, careful steps she slowly approached. When only a few steps away from the quivering grasses, she saw one of the parent birds desperately trying to hide one its chicks from her. It was very young – it must have fallen from the nest.

Holly knew the chick did not stand much chance of

surviving the night if it was still out of the nest, and she felt it was up to her to help if she could. The parent bird shrieked its protest and flew with a clatter of green wings to the high part of the trunk of a nearby beech tree from where, through bright yellow eyes, it watched Holly approach the chick.

Holly knelt in the grasses and gently cupped the chick in her hands, whispering words of comfort to it. She wasn't going to hurt it, she was going to try to help it, but what to do now? Holly looked up at the nest hole high up the gnarled tree trunk. After carefully placing the chick in her pocket, she began to climb up the tree. Slowly, one step at a time, Holly edged her way upwards. The dead wood of the trunk was rough against her fingers. A foolish glance towards the ground made her heart jump. It was a long way down. She was lucky in that there were lots of holes and knobbly bits to cling to.

When Holly reached the split in the trunk, she stood precariously in the wide gap and struggled to catch her breath. Then, legs shaking from tiredness, she climbed the remaining distance, and was able to carefully place the chick back inside the nest hole. At least two other fluffy bundles rubbed warm feathers against her fingers.

When Holly turned to climb down, she found herself suddenly face to face with the parent woodpecker on the tree trunk. It was still yelling its alarm call. It made her gasp when it flew very close past her, its wing feathers brushing her fingertips. Holly closed her eyes and turned her head away in case it pecked her. But nothing happened. As Holly dared to risk a look, the parent bird flew into the nest to rejoin its chicks, including the very lucky one!

As Holly carefully climbed down, if you had been there and looked very closely, you would have seen a kind smiling face, with lovely green eyes, within the leaves and branches. It was only there for a few fleeting seconds, and then as the breeze swayed the bright green leaves, it was gone. Holly didn't see it.

DEEP IN THE forest at the cold castle, the warlord was calling to his men to gather the dogs and get ready for a day's hunting. With the hounds baying excitedly, the troop of hooded men, armed with spears and bows and quivers full of sharp arrows, followed the warlord and entered the forest. So many animals had perished to these hunters in the past years that the woods around the castle were no longer home to many of the larger animals. These creatures lived in the forest further away from the castle. Even the birdsong was mostly absent, making the forest a dark, near silent and ominous place. If you only had one word to describe the forest around the castle, it would be, EVIL.

Soon the hunting dogs were in full cry. Before them a lone deer raced frantically away, rabbits with hearts beating dived down their burrows to safety and the few birds that dared to still live there stopped singing, as if holding their breath to see what would happen next.

But one creature didn't run away. The old bull aurochs, huge, black and muscular with wide, sharp tipped horns stood very still, sniffing the air, and twitching his ears to catch any new sounds that might spell danger. He was wary of the hunters, but not afraid of them. He had lived in these woods for nearly twelve summers and had come across this band of hooded hunters and their dogs before. Two of the hunting dogs and three of the hooded men he had met in the past would never hunt in these woods again.

Slowly he turned, then silently walked into the thickest bushes he could find. Better to be concealed and silent than run and make a noise he thought. The baying pack ran through the trees not too far from where the hidden aurochs silently stood, followed closely by the hooded men and the warlord.

The warlord was furious. After several hours of hunting, they had caught nothing – so empty of life had that part of the forest become. He shouted at his men to gather the dogs and head back to the castle. Slowly the hunting party trudged back through the forest towards the dark shape of the castle. It wasn't just the men who were looking dejected, even the dogs had lost their enthusiasm for the chase, walking with their tongues hanging out of their mouths, and with heads and tails down.

From his hiding place in the thick stand of bushes the old aurochs bull twitched his ears and nose as he sensed the hunters' return. They passed him by. He waited until the sounds of the hunting party had gone, then he emerged from the thicket and started feeding again.

3

SEARCHING FOR
A FRIEND

THE NEXT MORNING Holly was up early to do her jobs around the house and garden. First breakfast with her mother and father at the old but comforting wooden table. It had been made by her father and the years of family meals had worn grooves and hollows in its surface.

'Goodness me!' exclaimed her parents as they sat together around the table. 'What has woken you up so early this morning?'

'Well, today I am going to get the pet I have always wanted,' declared Holly.

Both parents looked a little shocked.

'Don't worry, you will like it because it will be small and won't cause any trouble at all!' she reassured them. Little did Holly know what was going to happen in the days and nights to come.

Her parents simply laughed, and said they couldn't wait to meet the new member of the family, whatever it was going to be.

AFTER BREAKFAST AND having completed her jobs, Holly went straight to her favourite part of the forest, and began to search very carefully, picking things up from the forest floor, inspecting them, and then discarding them if they were not exactly what she was looking for. Beneath one of the tallest trees in the forest, Holly found one of the very things she had been searching for. The tree she stood underneath was vast. It had dark crinkly bark and strange shaped branches covered in long green needles. It was a huge, tall pine tree, and it might have been THE tallest tree in the forest.

She bent down and carefully picked up what she had seen. Cupped in Holly's hand was a beautiful pine cone, shiny brown, fat at one end but tapering to a more pointed end at the other.

'This will do perfectly,' she hummed. Then she continued to search for more special things. After another hour of searching Holly had found almost all the things she needed; two pinky brown petals, two large shiny dark berries, one bright pink berry, four deer hairs and four little twigs, but she still needed a long pink flower stem.

Holly had been concentrating so hard on finding just what she wanted, that she had not noticed which way she had walked through the forest. Slightly confused she looked around, and no, she was sure she had not been in this particular part of the forest before. She wasn't afraid, since the birds were singing, the sun was shining and ahead of her the trees seemed to thin out to reveal a sunny glade. It looked very enticing ...

Holly walked forward to the edge of the trees then stopped. Peering over the top of a small bush she could see that ahead of her, washed in warm sunlight, was a beautiful flower strewn clearing, and at the far side of the clearing, a grassy mound covered with even more beautiful flowers swaying in the gentle breeze. To her amazement and delight, there amongst the flowers she could see a small deer, with its head down feeding.

Holly slowly and quietly moved from behind the bush and stepped into the clearing. Then, bathed in the warm golden sunlight, she walked ever so slowly towards the mound. The deer lifted its head, still munching the sweet grasses it was eating and without hurrying, turned and walked away in the opposite direction, disturbing two rabbits that had been sitting close by. The rabbits also hopped away as Holly began to walk up the grassy slope of the mound.

As she stood on the top of the flower strewn mound, the sun felt warm and comforting on her body, and the gentle breeze was just strong enough to move her long hair. Holly, being very inquisitive, explored the mound, which didn't take long since it wasn't very big. But she discovered it was of a very regular shape – it didn't look natural somehow – it was more like it had been made specifically to an exact shape, not by the wind and rain but by human hands.

Just one area of the mound was different. It became steeper and instead of grass it had a stone rockface with just a few flowers growing in the cracks between the rocks. Holly scambled down the grassy slope then turned to stand to look up at the steep rockface. Her eyes lit up. There in front of her was a lovely bright red flower with green leaves, and the long stem was pink – just what she needed.

Carefully Holly picked just one flower at the base of its long slim stem. It was perfect. All the things she had been looking for were now in her hand. Happily Holly climbed back to the top of the mound and sat in the flowers spreading her cape out in front of her and placing all the items she had found that morning on the folds of cloth.

Humming a happy tune Holly began to assemble the items, first two petals on the top of the cone on either side, then four little twigs spaced equally apart on the underside; the long pink flower stem was attached to the stubby end of the cone, while two big shiny dark berries pressed into place on either side of the cone just in front of the petals. The four hairs were pushed into the cone just where it narrowed to a point; and finally, the bright pink berry was placed right on the very tip.

'There,' said Holly, 'you're finished – my new little pet!'

Standing on four wobbly, twig legs on Holly's outstretched palm was a pine-cone mouse!

Holly laughed out loud when she looked at what she had created. She loved it, even though it did look a little wonky.

'Now,' said Holly, 'what do I call you? You are from a strong, tall pine tree and I'm sure you'll protect me from coming to any harm in these woods. So you need a name that will bring fear to anything that would try and hurt us.'

Holly thought some more, then suddenly exclaimed aloud to her new pet.

'I've got it, you'll be called Pinofita!'

(pronounced: p-no-fighter)

Holly got to her feet, and with Pinofita gently cupped in her hand, she looked around the grassy mound and the clearing in which it stood.

The whole scene still seemed strangely familiar, but she couldn't remember when or where she had seen it before. Then, with a glance upwards to see where the angle of the sun lay, she walked confidently towards the trees at the edge of the clearing, in the firm belief she would soon come across one of the many paths or trails she knew so well. At least that's what she hoped.

As the trees swallowed up Holly and Pinofita from sight, the smiling face with the kind green eyes appeared in the flowers on the grassy mound, but this time the smile was even more radiant and the face clearer. Several deer and rabbits reappeared on the top of the mound that Holly and Pinofita had just left, and overhead, the birdsong grew to a new crescendo.

Something in the woods had changed.

4

A DARK PLAN

DEEP IN THE forest that night the warlord sat in his large chair by the roaring fire and, before him, knelt three of his hooded men.

'Well,' he demanded, 'what of your search? What did you find and how far away was it?'

The first hooded man raised his stooped head and spoke in a gruff voice.

'I travelled north my lord and soon entered a place of higher ground. The tree cover was sparse and I could see high, snow-covered peaks.'

'What of the game?' yelled the warlord rudely.

'My lord,' the man continued, 'I saw small groups of a large kind of deer, red and black in colour with massive antlers.'

A cruel smile appeared on the warlord's dark veined face. 'I know of these creatures, they used to live much closer at one time.'

The hooded man stared silently at the warlord.

'Is that all?' the warlord demanded.

'No, my lord,' continued the hooded man, 'I didn't

see them, but I heard them, howling in the night —
wolves.'

'Wolves?' The reason for the tremble in the warlord's
voice was that these were the one animal he had a strange
fear of.

'They came close to where I camped but stayed
hidden in the trees away from my fire and out of my
sight. In the morning I came back here.'

'Did they follow you back here?' demanded the
warlord in a slightly wavering voice.

'No my lord, not that I know of,' replied the hooded
hunter.

As the silence grew the second hooded man raised
his head and began. 'My lord, I travelled to the East, but
soon the forest became so wet underfoot that walking
was difficult, the trees were much smaller and the land
didn't hold any deer or boar, only smaller creatures that
lived in the swampy, soggy ground.'

'Enough!' shouted the warlord.

He turned to the third hooded man and demanded
to hear what he had found. The third hooded man raised
his head and began his report.

'I travelled to the South and to the West my lord.
After two days travel, I became aware of signs of the forest
being worked by man's hand. Trees cut, the branches
being stacked for gathering and new saplings planted.

'Further on there were signs of well-worn paths and,
from a rise in the land, I could see smoke rising. Going
closer, I found a cluster of small timber and thatched
houses and, to one side of the village, land had been
cleared with crops sown and a few pigs rooting in the

small enclosures made for them. However, the woods were full of game – fat deer, wild pigs and lots of smaller game.'

'Well done,' said the warlord, 'go now, eat and rest, for tomorrow we begin our task of removing these unwanted villagers.'

As one the three hooded men stood up and left the great hall. The warlord rose and, after gathering a burning log from the fire, went to two large wooden doors set in the stone wall. He opened one of the doors, but nothing was revealed as the room was in a dank and oppressive darkness. Reaching up with the burning log he lit a straw torch resting in a frame fixed to the wall. Immediately a weak yellowy light illuminated the room. The warlord smiled a cruel smile and, as he moved forward, he laughed.

'Well, my old quarry, did you hear that? Your family seem to be living in the woods and snow north of here, with only the wolves for company.'

The laugh grew louder as he reached out his dark veined hand to roughly touch the cold head of a preserved stag standing alone in the middle of the cold room.

The stag was a massive creature, magnificent still, even in death, with a full rack of antlers that glistened in the weak light and dark eyes that seemed to blaze with anger at the fate he had suffered. With one last rough touch of the stag's head the warlord turned, dowsed the straw torch and left the room slamming the door behind him, returning the stag to his dark, lonely, miserable prison.

The warlord returned to his chair and sat brooding as to what to do next. Would it be hunting the large red black deer in the north alongside the wolf pack, animals he had a deep fear of, or further south to the game-filled woods around the village? He needed the villagers gone, they had no right to be in what he regarded as his territory, but the question was how to do it?

He sat for some time in the glow of the fire, stroking the hilt of his dagger and thinking. Then, as the embers burned low, his dark veined face broke into a cruel smile. An evil plan was forming in his devious mind, a plan that entailed something he knew he could deliver to the villagers ... fear!

5

A BIRTHDAY WISH

OVER SUPPER, HOLLY'S parents asked if she had managed to find the pet she wanted. They were acting as if it was an everyday question but Holly could tell they were surreptitiously looking under the table and behind the chairs for a furry half-wild thing.

'I did,' she said, 'do you want to see him?'

'Yes, of course we do,' chorused her parents.

When Holly returned from her bedroom, where Pinofita had been placed on her pillow, she gently put the little handmade mouse on the table.

'Please say hello to my new pet Pinofita.'

Both Boda and Eryk clapped their hands, laughed, and said 'hello' to the new member of the family, as well as saying to Holly that she had made a lovely pet mouse, albeit a bit wobbly on the four twig legs!

Supper was ending when Holly's mother asked her what she wanted for her birthday in two days time. Holly was shocked as she had totally forgotten it was so close to her birthday.

'Well,' she said slowly after thinking for a moment. 'Something sturdy to wear for when I'm in the forest please.'

'If I can,' her mother replied, 'let's see what your birthday morning brings.'

That night Pinofita was placed next to Holly's pillow as Holly settled down for a good night's sleep in the knowledge that her new pet was watching over her.

'Night, night Pinofita,' said Holly.

But the little mouse didn't reply, it just looked at Holly with two big, bright dark berry eyes.

'Oh, I do wish you could talk,' whispered Holly, knowing that such a thing was impossible, since a little creature made from a pine cone, leaves, berries, deer hair, twigs and a flower stem could never talk.

For the next two days Holly took Pinofita with her everywhere. Into the woods on sunny walks, helping with all her jobs in the house and the garden. The jobs took longer than usual since Holly had to take care to put Pinofita somewhere safe, out of the way of the brush as she swept the floors and the garden paths. Holly felt so happy that she had someone to talk to and share her life with, even though Pinofita didn't say very much. In fact, he didn't say anything at all, but just being there made Holly so much happier.

On the morning of her birthday, Holly was up early and sitting at the table with Pinofita placed in the middle of the table in front of her. Her parents came in with the simple breakfast for the family and, after eating it, Holly was beside herself with excitement to see what present she would receive. Boda left the table then came back with a package wrapped in cloth. Placing it in front of Holly, both parents wished her a happy birthday and watched as she reached to open the folded cloth. Holly's heart leapt when she saw a new pair of handmade trousers.

'Oh, thank you they're perfect,' she said happily, lifting up the trousers to admire them.

As she raised the trousers clear of the wrapping cloth, a small package of folded leaves fell onto the tabletop. All three of them stared at the little parcel in amazement.

'I have no idea what that is,' stammered her mother, 'it's not part of your present from us.'

'No, I've no idea where that came from,' said Eryk.

'We didn't put it there,' her parents said together, their voices hesitant and sounding confused.

Holly carefully picked up the package of leaves, gently holding the strange leafy bundle and turning it over and over in her hands.

'Are you going to open it?' Boda said in a quiet voice.

With eyes bright with excitement, Holly reached for the outer leaf of the mysterious package.

She carefully unwrapped the first leaf then, as she put it to one side in readiness to take the second leaf off, her mother's voice stopped her.

'Look there's some tiny writing on the leaf.'

Holly put the leafy package down and picked up the first leaf. Squinting, because the writing was so small, she read the tiny words.

'Sprinkle me on a friend and make a silent wish.'

Holly's mother and father reread the message, and both said again they had no idea what it meant, or how it had come to be within the folded trousers. Holly reached for the small bundle of leaves and carefully unpeeled the second leaf. Then, after four leaves had been unpeeled and placed gently on the top of the old wooden table, a fifth leaf was exposed. But this leaf was different, it was a golden coloured leaf that seemed to glow!

Taking the little package very carefully in her left hand Holly slowly unfolded the golden leaf to reveal some strange grains of golden powder, almost pollen-like that shimmered and glowed in the morning sunlight.

'Please read the message again, Mother,' said Holly in a small, strangled and very quiet voice.

Boda did and, in a whispered gentle tone, she read aloud.

'Sprinkle me on a friend and make a silent wish.'

Holly nodded and, after carefully placing Pinofita closer to her, she took the golden leaf and slowly tipped all the shimmering powder over the little pine cone mouse. Then, with her eyes tightly closed, Holly made her silent wish, a wish so precious that it made her squeeze her eyes really tightly shut. So tight a small tear emerged from between her long brown eyelashes and slowly trickled down her cheek. After a few seconds Holly couldn't bear it any longer and, opening her eyes stared at the hand-made mouse in front of her. Pinofita was still standing on his twiggy legs but there was no trace of the shimmering powder.

Disappointedly Holly looked at her parents, she wanted to cry. Her wish had been silent, and it really was all she wanted in the whole wide world. After a few more agonizing seconds Holly spoke quietly.

'Well, it isn't going to work is it?' And, turning her head away, tears began to run silently down her red cheeks. Her mother shared an agast glance with Eryk.

'Wait,' said Eryk, in a strange, gruff and trembling whispered voice, 'look, look at the mouse!'

Holly dried her eyes and turned her attention back to where Pinofita stood on the table. Pinofita was still standing on his wonky twig legs, he still had a pink nose, deer hair whiskers, big shiny berry eyes, pink petal ears, a flower stem tail and a gleaming pine cone body, but now there seemed to be a tiny dot of bright light within the pine cone.

Holly and her parents all held their breath as the light grew bigger and brighter. It kept growing until the brightness was so bright they all had to close and cover their eyes as the strange golden light filled the small room. After several seconds the light subsided and Holly opened one eye and looked cautiously between her fingers, then shrieked with delight causing her parents to open their eyes.

To their total amazement there on the table sat a brown mouse with a pink nose, ears and tail, big bright black eyes and twitching whiskers.

Pinofita was alive!

Holly still had her hand on the table from when she had tipped the shimmering powder over Pinofita and, it was to this hand, that the little mouse walked towards with a slowly swishing tail. Pinofita climbed onto Holly's hand and, after wrapping his tail around his brown furry body, he settled down to sleep. He was warm and soft. No one could speak. Holly gently cuddled Pinofita and let the little mouse rest.

'I'm going outside for a moment,' she said, and rose from the table then walked out into the morning sunshine in the garden.

With the sleeping Pinofita safely cupped in her hands, Holly raised her face to the sky and, with her eyes tight shut, she said thank you to whoever, or whatever, had made this happen.

In her room that night, Holly got ready for bed, all the time being watched by her new friend from his special place on Holly's pillow. All day her parents had talked about the strange leafy package, which had somehow disappeared and wondered where it might have gone and, more importantly, where it might have come from.

They had talked about the fantastic result of sprinkling the shimmering powder onto Pinofita. Even though they had seen the little mouse on Holly's lap, it still seemed an impossible thing to have happened. Only one possible explanation kept coming back to Holly, an explanation that was so very hard to accept, something she had never believed in before. Magic.

Even saying the word in her head made Holly tingle with excitement.

Now, tucked up in bed with the candle blown out, Holly snuggled down with Pinofita curled up warmly near her neck.

Through the window the kind face with the green eyes that materialised in the moonlit sky smiled down on the two happy friends, although Holly didn't see it.

Half asleep and happier than she had ever been, Holly whispered, as she had done every night since making her small friend, 'Night, night Pinofita.'

'Night, night Holly,' squeaked Pinofita.

Holly's eyes flew wide open!

6

THE TALL PINE TREE

BELOW HOLLY'S BEDROOM, her parents were lying awake in their bed, holding hands and staring up at the rough thatch ceiling roof through the darkness of the night. They were still awake when the early light of the dawn slowly crept into the room. Did that really happen they kept asking each other, and how can a mouse made from such simple things as a pine cone, deer hair, berries, petals, twigs and a flower stem actually come to life?

What they hadn't considered was that all these items that had made Pinofita, had once been alive themselves in the forest. And whilst it might not have been the same experience of life they knew, to those various items, it was still the joy of life. And all things alive try to stay alive, come what may. Sometimes all it takes is one special ingredient to resurrect that spark of life.

'Well,' said Boda, 'one thing is certain.'

'What's that?' asked her drowsy husband.

'There is no way we can tell any of the villagers. In fact, no one at all can know what has happened apart from the three of us.'

'If you say so,' said her husband, 'but you had better tell Holly before she goes out into the village and tells everyone.'

In fact Holly had had that very same thought herself, except her conclusions meant not even telling her parents her new mousy friend could talk. Not yet anyway. So strange and exciting did that sound that Holly repeated it in her head to herself. Her new soft, brown, furry mousy friend could talk! The tingly exciting feeling rippled through Holly's whole body again and again.

As the family gathered for breakfast – with Holly's parents sitting in their usual places at the table and Holly sitting at hers, but with a little wooden plate for Pinofita, made earlier by her father, alongside Holly's plate – it was strangely silent as there was no chatter or laughter. Holly sensed something was different and, turning to her mother, looked questioningly at her.

'Why are we so quiet this morning?'

Smiling at her daughter Boda replied softly, 'We have been awake all night thinking and talking about what happened yesterday and would like you to make us a promise.'

Holly panicked, did this promise mean having to let Pinofita go? She pushed this awful thought from the front of her mind and instead replied, 'And what is this promise you want me to keep?'

Holly then held her breath and waited.

'Well,' continued her mother, 'we both feel it would be better – for all four of us – if you didn't tell anyone in the village about where Pinofita came from. Just say, if asked, that he is a mouse you found in the forest that has become your tame pet. Could you do that please?'

With a huge smile of relief on her face, Holly reassured both her parents that she could easily do that, and yes, she agreed with them it would be awkward, in fact very, very awkward if the truth ever did come out. Both parents said thank you to their smiling daughter, and then conversation around the table began, as normal, at a breakfast time. The only one not to talk was Pinofita, since he had also made a promise – he had agreed with Holly not to talk unless he was sure only Holly could hear him. He sat quietly on the table munching away at his acorn with his whiskers and tail twitching.

'So,' said Eryk, 'and what will you two be doing this fine sunny day?'

Holly hugged herself at the sound of the word 'two', then thought for a moment and replied, 'To the forest, for Pinofita to get to know his way around as I do.'

'That's fine,' said Holly's mother, 'just take more care than usual, and don't let Pinofita get lost!'

'As if I would!' laughed Holly.

Once out in the woodland and perched on Holly's shoulder, Pinofita could hardly believe what he was seeing, smelling and feeling. Highest of all above him there was a wonderful blue and sunny sky with white fluffy clouds, and below that, vast numbers of trees towered overhead causing the sun beams to come and go. In addition the soft breeze brought new smell after new smell to his twitching nose, and his big ears were full of new and exciting sounds.

'Where are we going?' he squeaked in Holly's ear.

She smiled and replied, 'To a special place.'

Then she added slowly, 'It is special to me, but it is even more special to you.'

'Me? How is it special to me?' enquired Pinofita, so excited he nearly fell off Holly's shoulder.

'Wait till we get there,' said Holly in a quiet almost serious voice, 'then I'll explain.'

The two friends carried on chatting as they made their way through the corridors of oaks, beeches and pines, Holly being very careful not to slip or jolt Pinofita so he wouldn't fall. After a while Holly stopped, and said in a quiet voice, 'We're here.'

Pinofita looked around and saw many types of trees, bushes and flowers, all with a different smell and his ears were full of bird song from so many different kinds of birds. Then he looked in the direction Holly was looking, straight in front of them. He looked, and then his head began to lift up and backwards as he tried to see the top of the huge tree in front of them.

Holly reached up and lifted Pinofita gently off her shoulder and, holding him in her cupped hands, she slowly lowered herself into a sitting position on the soft leaves and needles of the forest floor.

With Pinofita sitting upright on the palm of her hand he could look directly into Holly's eyes and the two of them just gazed at each other for a moment in silence.

'Why is this place so special?' he squeaked.

'Because this is where most of you came from.'

Holly let that sink in. Then she lifted her head. 'Your body and head came from this very tree.'

'Oh!' whispered Pinofita, following her gaze. The

pine tree seemed never ending to him. As his eyes ran up the massive trunk, Pinofita felt a strange feeling inside his body, more of an urge really than a feeling, so he looked back towards his friend.

'Holly, please would you put me down so I can go closer to the tree?'

'You will come back to me won't you?' asked Holly, with a small tremor in her voice.

'Of course,' Pinofita reassured her. Then added seriously, 'You know I will.'

Holly smiled a nervous smile and, trusting what her tiny friend had said, carefully lowered her hand so Pinofita could jump down onto the forest floor.

Once on the ground Pinofita scurried over the leaves on the forest floor. When he arrived at the point where it grew out of the earth, he stood on his back legs and reached up the trunk as far as he could. In truth, this wasn't very high up the massive trunk, but it was as high as Pinofita could reach.

Holly watched in keen anticipation, as she feared he might climb up the tree where she could not follow. But instead, her furry friend stood motionless against the tree trunk, with the exception of his tail that slowly swayed from side to side. Then, he stilled, with his two front paws resting against the rough bark, and closed his eyes.

Watching him like a hawk, Holly thought she could see small, tiny blue flashes of light, like the smallest stars ever, around his two front paws. But the sunshine was so bright she couldn't really be sure she had seen what she first imagined she had.

After several minutes of standing perfectly still

Pinofita opened his eyes, shook his head as though he had just woken up, backed away from the tree, and then on all fours quickly ran back to where Holly anxiously waited.

Once back in Holly's cupped hands Pinofita sat in silence for few moments then said quietly, 'I feel different Holly.'

'How do you feel different?' his worried friend asked, her eyes widening in growing concern.

'Before going to the tree I felt small, but now I feel I could be much larger than I am.'

Holly giggled gently, 'As big as the pine tree?'

'No,' said Pinofita, 'just bigger.'

'Well, that's a lovely feeling to have,' said Holly, 'but for now you are perfect the way you are.'

With that Holly put Pinofita back on her shoulder and, turning from the pine tree, they set off walking down the secret animal trails with Holly telling Pinofita how to follow the faint tracks, just in case he ever needed to find his own way back to Holly, if they ever became separated. Holly never thought for one moment that she and Pinofita would ever be separated, it was too horrible a thought.

THE CASTLE OF the warlord was a hive of activity. Behind the wooden outer stockade, the warlord shouted orders to his hooded men who hurried about their tasks in preparation for their trek south. Earlier that morning the warlord had given orders to his assembled men.

He spoke to them of the great variety of animals that lived in the green woods to the south, and what rich hunting that would provide for them all. Every single one of the hooded men grinned their cruel grins and looked at one another with nodding heads. They liked the sound of what they heard. Then the warlord's tone changed as he began to speak of the problems that existed in those woods.

There was a village in the woods to the south with many villagers, men, women and children. They were working in the forest, his forest, and turning part of it into small fields for crops and their animals. The warlord continued to address his hooded men in a loud, commanding voice.

'These people are a nuisance to us, and they should not be there. Their farms drive out the wild animals.

Their changes to the forest make the hunt harder for us. We must make them leave the village and their crops immediately, and this is where you, my mighty hunting men, will bring something to each and every one of the villagers to achieve that.'

All the hooded men looked at each other with quizzical looks on their scarred faces; how could hunters do anything with crops and fields, and what were they supposed to bring to the villagers?

Raising his voice even more, the warlord cried, 'You my army of strong men with your sharp spears, arrows and swords, together with our wild hunting dogs will bring something to the villagers they are not prepared for.'

The warlord paused to take an extra big gulp of air and then, with his lungs full, he yelled out with all his might, *'Fear!'*

The word bounced around the stone walls of the great hall and echoed in the ears of the men standing in front of the warlord. The black veins on the warlord's face swelled with the effort of shouting, and made his whole face stranger and more evil than ever. In the silence that followed, the idea slowly sank into the minds of the hooded men, and they finally understood, causing their mouths to twist into cruel smiles again, but now they all had a new savage glint in their eyes.

'They are nothing,' shouted the warlord, 'just weak families of a few men but mainly women and children, that cannot possibly stand against all of us.'

The hooded men with their horrible grins believed what their master said since how could a band of villagers, the majority being women and children, stand in their way? They stamped their feet on the cold flag stones and raised their arms high over their heads shouting out a single word loudly in a chant.

'FEAR, FEAR, FEAR …'

7

THE FIRST
SECRET GIFT

HOLLY AND PINOFITA were wandering happily in the woods, talking and laughing together like old friends as they slowly walked the trails and paths through the trees and bushes. Overhead birdsong was all around them and a blackbird close by took flight through the low branches calling loudly.

Holly said quietly, 'I wish all the birds were like you.'

'Like a mouse?'

Holly laughed. 'My friends. I've been very kind to all the animals and birds I've met in these woods. But they still fear me.'

'Well,' said Pinofita tenderly, 'maybe not you especially, but people. Some people they have come across have tried to catch or hurt them, that's why they are afraid and call out their warning calls, like the blackbird did just a few moments ago. That is what they feel they have to do to be safe.'

'You sound like you know what they're saying,' said Holly.

Pinofita looked at Holly. 'Since touching the pine

tree, things within me have felt different. I told you about my new feeling of being bigger than I really am. Well, also, I can now understand what all the other creatures are saying.'

'Oh my!' gasped Holly in an awed whisper, 'what a wonderful gift to have.'

A silence grew between the two friends as they moved through the trees. The silence was broken when Holly spoke in hushed tones to her little furry friend.

'Would you try to do me a huge favour, please?'

'Anything,' replied Pinofita.

'If you can,' said Holly, 'please tell the birds and animals I would never hurt them and not to be afraid of me. Could you do that please?'

Pinofita smiled and nodded his little brown furry head. 'Of course I will – at least I'll try.'

The little brown mouse sat on Holly's outstretched hand and, closing his eyes he seemed to be falling asleep again, but that was far from the truth. In his mind Pinofita thought only of Holly's request and thought so hard about it that it seemed to grow and grow. The thought was getting so big that it was too big for his head or his body. His thought moved like a sunbeam through the forest canopy and into the sky where it rested like a pale golden cloud. Then the cloud burst and fell back to earth in tiny golden droplets of the finest golden mist.

Every one of those tiny drops of light held Holly's heartfelt request and, as they fell, they landed on passing flying birds and below them onto the bodies of other birds, animals and insects in the forest below and they all understood the message from Pinofita.

Pinofita slowly opened his eyes and found he was looking into the rather concerned face of Holly.

'What was that?' she asked in a very subdued and hesitant voice. But before Pinofita could reply, above them the plaintive mewing call of a buzzard rang out repeatedly as it circled high overhead.

The circles of flight became wider and wider as the large bird rose from the forest canopy, and his strong call carried Pinofita's message far and wide.

They both looked up and then Pinofita grinned at Holly. 'I think things will be different for you now.'

With a glowing feeling that seemed to pulse through all her body, Holly gathered Pinofita in a cupped hand and placed him in the folds of her hood. Following the path towards home, Holly noticed that there were no warning calls from frightened birds. Also, two small deer looked at them from nearby bushes but didn't turn and run; they just lowered their heads and continued feeding. Holly saw this new behaviour in the creatures and smiled one of her happiest ever smiles. Deep down she felt she was now really part of the green forest.

8

AN EVIL MESSAGE

MOVING SLOWLY BECAUSE of the weight of the supplies they carried, including the heavy skin tent they had brought for the warlord to sleep in at night, the war party continued on its way south through the forest. Each man carried a sharp spear, some also had swords whilst others had bows and a quiver of arrows slung over their shoulders.

Four men carried supplies piled high on stretchers made from two strong wooden poles with netting lashed between them. All the hooded men spoke to each other in gruff, animated voices about what was to come in the next few days. The hunting dogs, now on leashes to prevent them running ahead, bayed loudly as they felt the excitement and anticipation of the men.

At the head of the war party, the warlord too was filled with a cruel pride in what he and his band of men and dogs were setting out to do. He did not feel for one moment what he was doing might be wrong. After all he considered these woods to be his, and the villagers had no right to be living in them. In his mind he felt that whatever befell them, they had brought it upon themselves. He smiled a twisted smile as he thought that, in just two or three days, they would all be gone from his forest domain. After all, what could a group of a few men and women and their children offer in a form of resistance to his band of armed men – nothing, he thought smugly to himself, nothing!

If, soon after leaving the castle, the men had bothered to be more watchful, and to cast their gaze from side to side instead of just blindly heading south after their leader, they might have spotted some small movement in the bushes to their right.

The movement was the flapping ears of the bull aurochs as he swatted annoying flies away from his head whilst standing like a huge black rock within the leafy cover of his favourite hiding place. He had smelt the men and dogs approaching well before they came into sight, which gave him time to retreat to his green leafed sanctuary. His eyes narrowed at the sight of the passing men and dogs, less than the length of two tall pine trees through the trees from where he stood. His immediate instinct was to charge out of the bushes and into the column of hooded men causing as much destruction as his wide, sharp tipped horns and heavy cloven hooves could manage before they turned on him with spears and arrows.

His heart beat rose and his breathing became quicker as he readied himself. His front hooves were angrily scraping the debris of the forest floor, an action that usually happened just before he charged. His eyes narrowed and the bull was only seconds away from launching his attack when something happened that had never happened before to him in all his long years in the forest.

If you could have witnessed it you would have observed the bull aurochs, standing in the bushes pawing the ground with his front hooves, breathing quicker and beginning to move his mighty head from side to side. If you had been close enough to see that then you would have been advised to get away as quickly and as far as possible, or climb the nearest tree!

If you had stayed a few more seconds, you would have seen the enraged bull suddenly relax, to stop pawing the ground and slowly lower his head as if staring into the middle of the bush in front of him.

What had happened was so simple and yet it had such a devastatingly calming effect. An arm reached out from the bush in front of the aurochs, and the hand gently rested on the forehead of the bull, filling the animal with an inner feeling of calmness that immediately quashed his urge to fight. As the aurochs began to breath more slowly and deeply, he lowered his mighty head and found himself looking into the strange green eyes of a kind face within the leafy depths of the bush.

No words were spoken but, as the hand continued to rest on his head, the old bull understood what he had to do, but not when.

The hand withdrew from the bull's shaggy forehead and the image of the face in the bush grew faint then disappeared. Without a moment's hesitation the old aurochs stepped out from his hiding place and, at a safe distance, he began to follow the warlord's band of hooded men and dogs like a black avenging shadow moving steadily and silently through the trees.

9

A MESSAGE OF DOOM

A S THE DAY began to draw to a close, the hooded group of men were exhausted having walked much further than in a normal day's hunting and having had to carry lots of heavy supplies and fighting weapons. The warlord sensed their exhaustion so called a halt to the march when they entered a small clearing with a wide stream running through it that would offer them fresh, cool drinking water. The babbling waters would have also provided a refreshing place to bathe but that was something these men never really thought of. This meant they had a rather ripe smell of sweat that carried easily on the wind to any nose that had the misfortune to smell it.

One such nose that picked up this strong, pungent human scent belonged to something large and black like an avenging shadow moving steadily and silently through the trees some way behind the group, as it had been all day. The owner of this nose now understood his quarry had stopped for the night and so he would too. Breaking off from his task of following them, the old bull now grazed contentedly on some sweet grasses regaining his strength for whatever might come his way.

Back in the clearing, the warlord organised his men to make cooking fires, erect his tent and cook the evening meal, as well as securing and feeding the dogs. This they did, relieved to have a break from walking and carrying the heavy supplies. After the meal, the warlord sent four armed men ahead into the forest to scout out the lie of the land, to look for signs that they might be getting close to the village and, most importantly, to keep a watchful eye and ear open for any signs of wolves.

Cautiously, the four men walked into the woods in the direction the warlord had indicated. As night fell the forest sounds changed and, in the growing darkness, they became more shrill and, even for four grown men with spears, more frightening. Owl calls came eerily out of the darkness making all the men look up and around them just in case it wasn't an owl, but a strange wild creature of the night, or a forest witch that might attack them. They had never seen a forest witch, or any other witch come to that, but they had all heard horrible stories of these creatures.

Even the sounds of running animals crashing through the undergrowth also made them stop and grip their spears more firmly, their eyes wide and their hearts beating faster. These crashing sounds were made by small groups of deer and wild boar who, having been disturbed by the approaching men, all ran away in fear of their lives.

As the small group walked further south, now just over a half hour's walk from their camp, they heard another sound but this was something they recognised. It was a man's heavy breathing as though he was exhausted and struggling to find his way. They stopped to listen more carefully and to make sure it was only one person. Four of them against one tired traveller seemed safe enough for them to decide to move ahead quickly and intercept whomever it was out in the woods alone at night. Moving very quietly, they used the trees and bushes as cover to quickly get ahead of their quarry without being seen. Then they lay in wait behind two large tree trunks that stood either side of the animal track the night traveller was following.

Several minutes passed and then they heard the heavy, gasping breathing coming closer and closer. As the shape of the traveller came into view one of the hooded men stepped out in front and, swinging the heavy wooden shaft of his spear, hit the person on the shoulder sending him with a cry into a crumpled heap onto the forest floor. The sack he had been carrying fell with a thump.

The traveller was seized by two of the hooded men who tied his arms behind his back and sat him roughly against the trunk of a nearby tree. Another man searched eagerly inside the sack but found only some ragged clothes and a few meagre supplies of stale bread and meat that didn't smell very nice. The traveller, an old man, looked at his four captors through frightened eyes fearful of what would become of him.

'Who are you and where are you going?' questioned the leader of the four men, the one who had just hit the traveller with his spear shaft.

'I am just trying to find another village near here,'

stammered the old man.

'Why?' asked the hooded leader.

'Well, the village where I used to live was flooded by the nearby river and all the houses were either destroyed or damaged so badly they could not be repaired,' replied the man.

'So why not rebuild and stay in the village?' queried the leader.

'Too much damage and too many people left the wrecked village immediately, so those of us who remained were too few to make the village whole again. And the river might flood a second time. So, I moved on to try and find a different village, the one I believe is near here in the woods.' The old man spoke with a real sadness in his voice.

'Right,' commanded the leader in his gruff voice, 'on your feet and come with us.'

'Where to?' asked the frightened old traveller.

'You'll see when we get there,' laughed the hooded leader cruelly.

Supported by two of the hooded men on either side, the traveller was marched back through the forest to the camp by the stream. Once there, the men took their captive to the tent of the warlord and, as the warlord appeared from inside the tent of animal skins, the leader of the four men threw the old man roughly onto the ground.

'We found him wandering in the woods my lord, not far south of here. He says he is trying to find his way to the village we are travelling to,' reported the hooded leader.

With his hands on his hips, the warlord stood over the traveller who was still lying on the ground where he had been thrown.

'Well done,' said the warlord in his deep threatening voice, 'you did right to bring him back here to me.'

The hooded leader lowered his head in what looked like a bow to his master and smiled a grin that revealed at least four of his rotten teeth were missing.

From his position of lying on the ground, when the old man looked up it was as if he was looking at a giant, well, at least a medium sized one. The warlord placed one large foot on the back of the traveller's head pinning him even closer to the forest floor.

'I will let you continue on your way, on one condition,' hissed the warlord towering over the old man.

'Anything you ask my lord,' the old man uttered as best he could since leaves and pine needles were getting into his mouth making talking difficult.

In a thunderous voice the warlord continued, 'You can go free on the condition you promise to find the village you seek and tell all the villagers what you have seen here. My armed men, our wild hunting dogs and me! Tell them we are coming to burn their village to the ground and drive them out far from these woods, my woods. Do you agree?'

The old man agreed as vigorously as he could, given the leaves filling his mouth.

'Free him, take him back to where you found him and point him in the direction of the village,' bellowed the warlord who then turned on his heel and went back towards his tent. As he walked away from the old man, who was still lying prone on the ground, he heard the warlord say something under his breath to himself that made no sense whatsoever.

'Better to use this old man to increase the fear than waste my wish.'

So confused and terrified was the old man he immediately forgot the quiet words the warlord had muttered.

AN HOUR LATER the old man, still very shaken and frightened after his capture and ordeal, was now free and walking slowly through the moonlit night down the trail he had been shown. The trail was not wide and his progress was slow as he stumbled over tree roots and brambles tugged at his tattered trousers, but at least he was free. After a night walking as quickly as he could he felt his strength fading, but he gritted his teeth and kept going since he knew he had to warn the villagers. They had to get out of their homes before the horde of hooded men, the pack of dogs and their gigantic leader arrived at the village and set fire to it. He had to keep going he kept telling himself. Using up the last of his energy, he walked till he could not put one foot in front of the other and, with a few last faltering steps, he fell forward into the soft bed of leaves on the forest floor and surrendered to his exhaustion.

He was still on the forest floor the next morning, more

unconscious than asleep, when one of the woodland foragers found him. The forager, a youth named Edmund, was horrified when he saw the still body, as his first thought was to think the man on the ground was dead! Pushing his fear aside, Edmund knelt alongside the man and gently shook his shoulder. Nothing happened, so he tried again; this time making the shaking action much stronger. The man stirred and groaned. Edmund helped the old man into a sitting position and, after wiping away the leaves that had stuck to the man's face, he asked him who he was and what had happened to him. The poor man could hardly talk since his throat was so dry and his voice so cracked.

Edmund spent most of his working days exploring the forest looking for things he could collect and take back to the village. Lovely things to eat such as honey and berries, including special roots and flowers that he could trade for bread and oatcakes. Last night Edmund had slept in one of his woodland dens made from branches propped against a tree trunk, not as comfortable as the empty cottage he sometimes used in the village, but much better than sleeping under the stars especially when it rained.

Edmund was also a well-prepared forest forager since he carried a skin water bottle fastened to his belt. He reached for the skin bottle and, having removed the wooden stopper, gently held the open end to the old man's lips. Slowly, the life-giving water ran into the waiting mouth. The old man spluttered and choked with the first mouthful, but then he recovered and drank slowly and deeply. Finally the old man revived enough to wipe his mouth with the back of his hand and look into Edmund's kind but worried eyes.

'You asked me who I am and what am I doing in the forest?' croaked the old man in a weak voice.

'Yes, I did,' replied Edmund nodding his head, 'but don't talk now if it's too much effort. Let's try and get you to the safety of the village or at least to where my friends are working in the forest about two hours' walk from here.'

The old man raised a thin hand and shook it.

'No,' he said weakly, 'I am Gwillam but who I am and why I am in the forest alone doesn't matter, what does matter is that I have a message for you and the rest of the village that you all must heed. Your very lives depend upon it!'

Edmund's eyes grew wide with apprehension – what on earth could Gwillam know that had such importance for himself and all the villagers?

Gwillam continued to tell Edmund the account of what happened to him the previous night. Of travelling in the forest to find a new home, being captured, taken to a strange camp full of armed men, wild hunting dogs and led by a gigantic leader who was coming to burn the village to the ground and to drive all the villagers away, out of his woods.

'That's the message I have for you,' he said in a faltering voice, 'please go quickly and deliver the message to the village. Get out while you can.'

Edmund was appalled at the horror of the message, especially the description of the armed group coming to carry out the threat. He thought quickly about what to do and then, having made up his mind, he looked down at the old traveller.

'Right Gwillam, you are coming with me. Your message will have more weight if you tell the story rather than me.'

'No,' protested the traveller, 'I will slow you down, go now and run like the wind to your friends, tell them and then get away.'

Edmund would have none of it, he was not leaving an old man in the forest alone, so he helped him to his feet and then, with one arm supporting him, Edmund led them south, just as fast as they could walk. It took all Edmund's strength to keep them going as Gwillam was weak and couldn't walk very fast. In the end Edmund, being a strong youth, put him over his shoulder and, carrying him, he trotted along the trail at a much faster pace. He needed to get to where Holly's father and the other forest workers were since that meant a bit more security and strength in numbers as Edmund had no idea how close the armed group coming to burn the village were behind him.

10

TERROR COMES TO THE VILLAGE

EVERY RUSTLE OR noise from the forest bushes and thickets that they passed caused Edmund to catch his breath nervously as that might have signaled the presence of an armed man. Edmund would have been far more relaxed on his journey south if he had known that all the hooded armed men and their leader had only just packed up their overnight camp and begun their relentless trek south.

The warlord was in a foul mood as he had spent a sleepless night on his narrow travelling bed, which was the most uncomfortable bed in the whole world. His only comfort was the thought of the old man taking his message of destruction to the villagers ahead of their arrival. That would plant the seeds of fear in the villagers' minds ahead of the armed group coming within sight of the village. He grinned at the thought of what he imagined their reactions were going to be. They would run round scared out of their wits and not know what to do; they would scream and cry out in terror and, hopefully, they would leave their small houses and run away into the forest even before he arrived to set those homes on fire.

As the warlord's armed group set off, so too did the immense black shadow in the trees that followed at a safe undetected distance. If the warlord had known what was silently trailing them, he would not have been grinning so broadly that morning.

IT TOOK EDMUND over two hours of exhausting travel through the trees following the trail south before he heard the sound of men working in the forest ahead of him. Heartened by the sound of his fellow villagers, he made one last great effort and, as he staggered into the small clearing where four of the villagers were working, he fell forward with a cry unable to go any further.

All the men turned at the sound of the noise and they were taken aback at the sight of a boy with an old man over his shoulder falling to the ground. Immediately they all rushed forward to help. Holly's father was the first to reach them, and he and two others helped both the fallen men to sit up. They were shocked when they recognised Edmund and curious as to who the other, older man was and what had happened.

Water was brought to both men who continued to sit on the forest floor gratefully drinking. Eryk urgently asked Edmund what had happened and who the old man was. Edmund explained he had come across Gwillam earlier that morning lying flat on the ground as though he were dead and that, whilst he didn't know who he was, he was actually a messenger with terrible news for the village.

'A messenger?' exclaimed Holly's father, 'what message?'

Before Edmund could speak Gwillam raised his right hand and, looking at the men in front of him, he spoke in a weary voice.

'I am so sorry but the message I was told to give you is one of pain, horror and destruction.'

Holly's father and the other three foresters from the village all shared looks of disbelief and shock, then turned back to the old man.

'Go on then ... what's this message of doom?' one of the other men asked.

After the old man had told his story and given the cruel message from the giant leader of the armed party of hooded men, all the four men looked at each other but said nothing. A deep silence surrounded the small group, the only sound being that of birdsong in the trees and bushes. The first to react was Holly's father, who first stood then looked around at all the others before speaking.

'Right, we need to get these two back to the village, and to gather everyone together to decide what to do, and quickly as we don't have much time.'

The others nodded in agreement and, after helping the exhausted Edmund and Gwillam to their feet, they gathered their tools and then they all set off back to the village as fast as they could.

The last part of their journey through the green woodlands to the village, just before the place where the trees gave way to the fields of crops, was down a short but steep gully filled with large rocks and a few prickly bushes. They used the gully since the forest, for a long way either side, was very thick and choked with sharp thorn bushes and brambles. The six carefully made their way down the gully, calling to the villagers working in the small fields to follow them. They entered the village. Immediately people stopped whatever they were doing and began to gather around the group to find out what was going on. Holly's mother was amongst them.

The crowd stared in shock at the strange old man sitting on the ground and worriedly looked to their own foresters to explain why they had returned unexpectedly from their work. It was Edmund who spoke. He explained how he had found Gwillam in the forest that morning and that the old man carried a truly horrible message for the villagers. A warning of an approaching war band.

As he finished, Gwillam stood and cried out, 'You need to get out now before they arrive. Go, flee and save your lives and those of your children.'

The effort of speaking was too much for him and he collapsed once again onto the ground in front of the villagers. Edmund asked one of his friends to help him carry the old messenger to an empty cottage where he would look after him since there was nowhere else for him to go. Picking him up gently, they made ready to leave the group of villagers who were all now talking frantically about what would happen next and what they would have to do, when Holly's father spoke in a loud commanding voice.

'Wait,' he shouted, 'before we decide anything, go to your homes, gather all members of your family and whatever weapons or tools you have and we should all meet here again just before sunset. Then, hopefully, we can plan what to do.'

Most of the villagers nodded in agreement and the small crowd broke up with people walking quickly in different directions back to their homes. Holly's father and mother looked at each other and, with worried looks on their faces, both said at the same time, 'Where's Holly?'

11

A DEFENSIVE PLAN

HOLLY WAS SITTING at the table with Pinofita in front of her when her parents burst in.

'Oh, thank goodness you're here,' Boda said, 'we feared you might still be out in the woods.'

'What would be wrong with that?' asked Holly, who was usually not home until the sun set over the trees. Her parents looked at each other and then Eryk said very gently, so as not to frighten his daughter too much.

'We have a serious problem facing the village and we all have to go to a full village meeting to decide what to do.'

'What sort of serious problem?' asked Holly beginning to feel uneasy at the looks on her parents' faces.

'We'll know more when we get there,' said her mother, 'in the meantime come with me to the woodshed.'

'Why?' said a now very nervous Holly.

'For safety. Someone dangerous is coming. Please?' begged her mother, her face very pale and worried.

Holly quickly put Pinofita on her shoulder and followed her mother outside. When they reached the woodshed, her mother offered her two large wooden poles each having a blunt end and a sharp end, poles that were normally used to support saplings when first planted.

'Which one is the easier for you to handle?' her mother asked, her voice trembling and with a tiny tear trickling down her left cheek. Holly was now so frightened she stepped forward and put her arms around her mother and hugged her.

'What do I need this for?' asked Holly bravely.

Boda took a shakey breath, still holding the two poles in her outstretched arms. 'We have to be ready to defend ourselves, everyone has to be ready.'

Neither Holly nor her mother could see Pinofita who was now sitting in the folds of Holly's hood, but, if they had seen him, they would have a seen a mouse with every hair on its body sticking up, making him look bigger than ever.

Holly decided which pole suited her best by checking that, with the flat end under her arm, the pointed end just reached the ground. The shorter pole was easier to handle than the other longer one so that was the one she chose. Satisfied with her daughter's choice, Holly's mother took the other larger pole for herself and led the way back to the house where they found Eryk standing waiting for them wearing his dark cloak and with his axe in one hand and an unlit torch in the other.

'Before we go,' he said softly, 'please put on your winter cloaks as we might be out for some time.'

Very carefully, Holly hid Pinofita in the folds of her hood. 'Don't let anyone see you,' she whispered.

Dressed in their heavier winter cloaks and, carrying their weapons and a couple of torches, the little family, set off to walk back to the village meeting place, joining other families on their way.

Once all the villagers gathered at the meeting, it became a loud babble of voices. Holly stood with her family on the fringe of the gathering, ears full of several heated conversations all happening at the same time; in short it was chaos. One loud voice shouted for quiet and calm. The owner of this voice was her father Eryk. She felt a jolt of awe as he stepped forward and stood in front of the assembled entire village; every man, woman and child including two babies who were being carried by their parents.

'Quiet everyone,' he said in his loud voice, 'we are not going to solve anything by having everyone talk at the same time. What we need are suggestions as to what to do next to defend ourselves.'

One man suggested they should run away before the armed men arrived. Another voice called for everyone to go home and wait to defend their own houses when the horde came. Standing very close to her mother, Holly was deafened by the noise. Her mother put her arm around her and gave her a quick reassuring squeeze.

At the centre of the crowd, Holly's father listened to these ideas then, raising the axe in his hand, he called for silence. 'No. I say we fight as a village not as individual families. Together we are stronger and we do not run away like scared foxes back to the woods. Who here agrees with me?'

Some voices agreed with him, but others shouted

support for running away now whilst there was time. The meeting began to deteriorate into just a noise of different ideas being shouted out and no common agreement as to what to do. Holly began to feel frustrated. The meeting was solving nothing, and these fearsome hunters were getting closer.

Then she felt the sudden loss of warmth as her mother quickly stepped forward and stood next to her husband.

'No!' Boda yelled, causing the villagers to cease their many conversations and to turn to look at her. When she saw she had their attention, she continued to speak. 'We have too much at stake here in our village to just run away and leave everything for these invaders to come and burn it down. We don't just have houses, we have homes. Homes where we have brought up our children, homes that shelter us and homes we have worked hard for.'

Another voice rang out. 'That's right, my Dan has made us a new table for our home and I ain't leavin' it here for it to be burnt by these thugs!'

'I was thinking in terms of people rather than furniture, but exactly right Ethel,' responded Boda with a smile, and then continued. 'But consider this, if we leave now as some of you have suggested, where would we go? Just ask yourselves, where would we go? The forest would be the only place for us, and we have neither shelter there nor supplies of food. If we leave our crops and animals now, we'll have no food to see us through the winter once all the berries are gone from the forest bushes. I for one will not surrender all the things we have built here only to starve later in the woodland. We must

69

defend ourselves properly with what weapons we have. We need a plan.'

'Yes, yes,' shouted the villagers with one voice. 'A good plan to beat these killer hunters, that's what we need.'

Holly saw her father's look of love and admiration for his wife who had found the words to bring the village together. Now it was his turn to talk. The plan he outlined to the villagers required them to form a wall of defense between the two houses which the attacking group would come to first. It would give the villagers who had skills with a weapon a chance to fight and turn back this onslaught. He also outlined several vicious traps.

Holly was slightly appalled to hear how easily they could plot such things but beside her, people were nodding in agreement; it seemed a good plan.

'What if the attackers come from a different direction to the one you have said. How will your plan work then?' another worried voice called out.

Eryk sighed and admitted that this would be difficult. He added, 'What we really need to know is what their method of attack is. Then we can be better organised to defend ourselves.'

The meeting broke up and the villagers with their weapons of axes, poles, stones, four bows and some arrows plus several short daggers took themselves off to their allotted places, ready to defend their village, their homes, their families and their lives. Holly's mind was full of worries and doubts, but what else could the village do – they were not going to just run away.

HOLLY SLIPPED THROUGH the darkened village with Pinofita sitting safely concealed in her hood. She had come to a decision. She was not going home with her parents. On hearing her father say, 'we really need to know what their plan of attack is', Holly had smiled a grim smile of determination and, gripping her pole even more firmly, she had quietly stepped back from the people around her and melted into the shadows of the nearby houses.

'What are you doing?' said the small voice by Holly's ear, 'where are we going?'

Holly didn't stop walking but replied quietly, 'You heard what my father said. We need to know what their plan of attack is and there is only one way that's going to happen and there are only two souls here tonight who can make that happen.'

'Oh!' exclaimed Pinofita, clinging on more tightly to Holly's hood as she broke into a run and headed off across the darkening crop fields towards the gully, and beyond the gully, the forest and beyond that, the approaching hunters.

12

THREAT OF DOOM ARRIVES

THE WARLORD'S GROUP had arrived in the clearing beyond the top of the steep gully. After a day of double-quick marching, they were totally exhausted but proud of their speed and the distance they had covered. The warlord had pushed them hard. The message of burning destruction should now have reached the village and he wanted to add to the terror by lighting fires at the top of a steep gully. The village lay still and silent below. His men would rest through the night in comfort and warmth, but those same fires would keep the village folk awake, trembling in their houses and exhausted by morning. He liked his plan and so stood to one side and waited patiently, something he didn't normally do, as his tired men erected his tent, then made the evening meal.

The eight dogs were worn out and, after eating their food, lay down on the grass in the clearing, tethered to short stakes and, with their heads resting on their front legs, they fell into a deep sleep under the gathering stars.

After his meal in his tent, the warlord sent for the hooded man who had scouted these woods and found the village for the first time. When the man entered the tent, he knelt on one knee in front of his leader awaiting orders.

'We are so close now,' the warlord said in a normal voice not shouting as he usually did, 'go now and find out what you can about how the villagers are preparing to defend the village and themselves or if they are going to flee. Any news will be good so go now, do not be seen and report back to me as soon as possible.'

The hooded man stood, bowed his head briefly then turned and, moving aside the heavy flap of the tent entrance, he disappeared into the growing darkness, stopping only to collect his spear.

RUNNING AS QUICKLY as the uneven ground would allow in the fading light, Holly made her way across the fields to the base of the gully. Pinofita was still clinging on inside her hood. On entering the gully, her breathing was heavy and laboured so, before trying to climb the steep slope, she waited by the side of a large rock and allowed herself to catch her breath. Looking back over the fields, she could see her village where a few lights burned normally from some of the windows. It might look sleepy she thought but she also knew it was anything but, as people would now be in their positions waiting for an attack to happen. This is so wrong she thought. Why does it have to be like this? What have we done to have such a horrendous threat made against us? To calm herself she whispered to her travelling companion.

'Are you all right Pinofita? Did you manage to hang on whilst I was running over the fields?'

Immediately an excited voice whispered back. 'I did, and it was very bumpy, but what are we going to do now?'

Holly thought for a minute and then said in a hushed voice, 'We do whatever it takes to get my father what he said he needed. We are going to try and discover what their attack plans are.'

'Sounds very dangerous,' replied Pinofita, then he added, 'we had better take extra care and not get caught because, if we are caught, then the village will never learn what the attack plans are.'

'I know,' said Holly seriously, 'but first we need to get to the top of this gully and see if these hunters have arrived here yet.'

With that she gripped her pole firmly and, using it as a support to aid her balance with her friend in her hood, she began to climb the gully to face whatever dangers they might meet at the top.

Holly was not even half-way up the gully when Pinofita squeaked urgently in her ear.

'Take cover Holly – someone's coming down the gully towards us!'

Holly had been concentrating so hard on keeping her footing in the darkness and not slipping on a loose stone that she had been looking down and not up and ahead.

Luckily a pair of bright, black eyes had been looking forwards to the top of the gully, and they saw the hooded figure carrying a spear as it stood at the top of the gully silhouetted against the rising moon before beginning its descent. Holly quickly and silently moved to the side of the path she had been following and sat in a huddle with her cloak around her to disguise her true shape, and to try and look more like one of the many rocks that lay along the length of the gully.

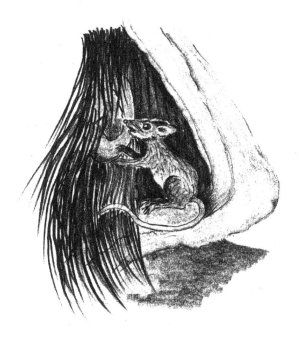

The sound of the approaching figure became louder and louder as it slipped and slid down the stony path. Holly and Pinofita both held their breath as the dark shape passed by and, without a moment's glance in their direction, it carried on down towards the fields and beyond that to the village.

Quickly Holly regained the path and, after few more minutes of climbing, reached the top of the gully. She was cautious. She didn't just walk out of the gully into the clearing she knew was there. Instead, Holly crawled to the side of the gully entrance and, from behind a small, twisted bush, looked fearfully out to see what lay before them.

What Holly and Pinofita saw made them both gasp in disbelief, for ahead of them at the far end of the clearing, just before the dark tree line of the forest began, they saw several small cooking fires and one tent that cast strange shadows in the light of the moon. Around the fires there seemed to be an army sitting, standing and walking around their camp.

'Oh Pinofita, the old man was right, but they are not just coming, they're here! So many of them to attack us and burn all our homes to the ground,' gasped Holly feeling frightened, small and dejected.

'There are lots of them,' said Pinofita peering out from under Holly's hood, his hair beginning to bristle again. 'But,' he continued, 'so many men, most moving round and casting lots of moving shadows make it easier for us. Our shadows will not easily be seen as we move closer.'

Holly smiled. 'Oh, you clever mouse, I feel a bit better now.'

But what both Holly and Pinofita hadn't seen, and therefore not taken into consideration, were the eight hunting dogs lying in the grass asleep and unseen to them on the other side of the tent. And hunting dogs have a very keen sense of smell, even when asleep.

Feeling reassured by her furry friend's words, Holly began to crawl towards the tent. Keeping low to the ground and in the shadow of the few bushes that grew in the clearing, Holly desperately tried to keep them both hidden from the many eyes in the camp. It was not a very long way to the tent, but it seemed ages to Holly since crawling on hands and knees is a very slow way to progress. The moon, normally something Holly loved to see, was also not being much help at that moment, as it hung high in the night sky and cast an eerie pale light that flooded the clearing.

Despite all this Holly continued to make her way slowly forward. Once she had to stop moving and quickly put her face into the grasses to make herself as small and as invisible as possible. That was when one of the hooded men left the main group and walked towards them. Holly's heart beat even faster and she held her breath waiting to be discovered, only for the man to stop short of where they lay, stoop to collect some dry branches and return to the camp to throw them on one of the fires.

'Oh my,' Holly whispered, 'I thought for a moment he was going to step on us.'

Pinofita said nothing because at that moment he was feeling very strange and didn't know why. It all began when the hooded man started walking towards them, and Pinofita feared for Holly's safety and wanted to defend her from whatever danger this hooded man posed. He felt the hair all over his body begin to bristle making him feel and look bigger and his eyes felt extremely hot.

He didn't understand it, but he was now calming down and feeling more like his old self.

If you had been able to see what had happened, you would have seen the little brown mouse grow bigger as the hair on his body stood up on end, and his two normally bright black eyes began to turn a deep red … making him look very fierce indeed.

Having recovered from her fright, Holly began to edge closer to the back of the tent. She wanted to be able to listen through the animal skins to whatever plots were being hatched inside. But before they could reach the dark safety of the rear wall, they saw a very large man come out of the front and call his men to him.

'Oh no!' exclaimed Holly in an exasperated whisper to Pinofita, 'that must be the giant leader the old man talked about. But he's going to talk to his men outside at the front of the tent and not in it. We daren't go closer or we'll be seen, but if we stay here, we won't hear what they are saying. What do we do Pinofita?'

The little mouse thought quickly for a moment. 'If we could get inside the tent and use it as cover then we could get very close to where the leader is standing and then be able to hear everything – without being seen.'

'Oh, good idea!' exclaimed Holly, almost too loudly.

'Shhh,' warned Pinofita, 'not so loud. Someone might hear you.'

In a whisper Holly apologised and then started crawling forward again to the back of the tent. Very soon they got there and Holly sat with her back resting against the rough skin. She was relieved to stop crawling as her knees were aching as well as being wet from the grass and there was a small trickle of blood running down her leg from a cut on her knee, caused when she had knelt on a sharp stone edge.

Listening carefully, they could hear the sound of a loud voice, but the tent was preventing them from hearing the words clearly. Holly tried to lift the bottom edge of the tent, only to find it was securely fastened to the ground to stop any wind or rain blowing in to disturb the large occupant when he was asleep.

'I can't lift the side much,' said an exasperated Holly, as she tried desperately to lift the firmly secured animal hide.

'Let me see,' squeaked Pinofita jumping down off Holly's shoulder onto her knee, then with another small leap to finally land on the grass.

'Try again,' he urged Holly.

Taking a firm grip on the bottom edge of the tent and a really deep breath, Holly summoned all the strength she had and pulled upwards. After a few moments the weight and resistance of the tent was too much for Holly, and the edge of the tent dropped to rest firmly on the ground again.

'See,' said a breathless Holly, 'I can't lift it very high.'

'High enough,' said a faint voice from inside the tent.

'Pinofita, no!' exclaimed Holly in a voice louder than she meant. 'Come back out here now, *please.*'

The words of the small voice from inside the warlord's tent did nothing to calm Holly. 'I'll be fine, you stay there to let me out, and don't make a noise whilst I go and try to hear what they are saying.'

For Holly time almost stopped. The seconds seemed like minutes and the minutes dragged on like hours. Keeping her ears and eyes open for any warning sounds or shadows moving towards her, Holly sat and waited, and waited. It seemed like an eternity.

After about only five minutes, that seemed to Holly to have been so much longer, she heard the men at the front of the tent all shout out with a great cheer. Holly was terrified.

'What on earth did that mean? Has Pinofita been seen and captured?' she gasped aloud. But before Holly could imagine any more horrible thoughts about what might have happened to Pinofita, she heard a gruff voice from inside the tent that made her blood run cold.

'Bring me some water and light my torch in here.'

Holly felt sick with worry; the huge leader was now back in his tent and when the torch was lit, surely he must see her friend. As a deep despair grew inside her, a small voice by the tent edge near where she sat urgently called to her.

'Holly, Holly please lift the tent edge and let me out before the torch is lit and they discover me in here.'

She tried to do as she had been asked but when Holly attempted to lift the tent edge, this time it hardly moved. It was so heavy. The more she tried and failed the more she panicked. No matter how hard she pulled she could not lift up the tent edge. Tears of frustration and worry began to well up in her eyes as she imagined what awful fate would befall her tiny, furry friend.

However, what made it even worse was now her

fingers were so sore from trying to lift the heavy skin tent side that it was really painful to try. Holly never thought of giving up, but she began to struggle to see what she could do to save her little furry friend Pinofita from being discovered. In her anger with herself for not being able to lift the tent edge she slapped both hands onto the grass in frustration.

'Ouch!' cried Holly – just about managing to suppress the loudness of her cry, as the already sore fingers on her right hand slapped down on something round and hard hurting them even more. The sharp-ended pole that her mother had given her earlier that evening was resting in the grass where Holly had dropped it.

Immediately Holly seized the pole with both hands and scrambled to her feet. And then carefully inserted the sharp end under the tent edge. Once the pole was in place, she stood with legs apart and knees bent and, using all the strength she had, slowly pulled the blunt end of the pole up to the height of her trembling knees.

It worked!

Slowly but surely the tent edge lifted, and a brown furry body ran out of the tent to Holly. With the pole in her right hand and Pinofita on her shoulder she cast caution to the wind and ran ... not crawled, from the back of the tent to the cover of the bushes that lay on the way back to the gully.

They had almost reached the first bush when the silence of the night was shattered by the loud baying of the hunting dogs.

13

GOTCHA!

HOLLY THREW HERSELF onto the ground almost catapulting Pinofita out of her hood and into the grass. Fortunately, Pinofita had strong claws and was able to grip onto Holly's cloak so he wasn't thrown forward.

'Oh no!' Holly cried softly to Pinofita, 'they have dogs, who must have smelt or seen us, and they will now come after us and catch us. I didn't know there were dogs in the camp.'

They were now only a short distance from the safety of the gully, but the camp was in uproar with hooded men running everywhere and the huge leader shouting orders to find out why the dogs were barking. 'Why are they barking?' the warlord shouted – 'is it wolves near the camp?' His voice couldn't cover the fear in it as he asked this question.

There was so much activity and so many men running around looking for whatever had disturbed the dogs that it was not safe to move. So they didn't, they just lay still as stone in the grass expecting to be discovered at any moment. Keeping still was scary, but it was safer than running away and risking being seen and captured.

The men nearest to where the dogs were tethered were looking frantically all around to see what might have caused them to wake and howl. They saw nothing and, despite the efforts of the entire camp, they could find no reason why the dogs were howling and continued to howl even when the men tried to calm them.

If the men had had the same keen sense of smell as the dogs, they would have understood the fear that was causing the constant howling.

Fear that the dogs themselves were experiencing because they all recognised what the smell was!

The source of the scent that had woken and alarmed the dogs stood silent and motionless on the edge of the dark tree line, some way behind the warlord's camp. The moonlight cast deep shadows in the clearing but, amongst the trees, there was no light, just a wall of blackness and, within this dark sanctuary, completely hidden from the people in the camp, stood the even darker shape of the black bull aurochs, his journey nearly over and his task soon to be completed.

The longer time went on and they were still not found, the more relaxed the brave pair became and the easier their quiet conversation became.

'So,' asked Holly, 'what did you hear, and do you know how they plan to attack the village?'

'I think so,' squeaked Pinofita, 'they believe the village cannot defend itself against them, and that most of the families will leave by the morning. The leader is very confident and wants to march straight down into the village and take control of it.'

'Oh, that's good,' smiled Holly, 'that way they will walk straight into the trap that my father has set.'

'Not exactly,' continued Pinofita, 'they are only going straight to the village with half the men. The other men and all the dogs will go around the fields and into the village from the other side, near where we live.'

Holly imagined what that meant and then gasped aloud. 'Oh no, that way all the villagers will be trapped between the two groups. We have to get back and tell my father so he can do something to stop them.'

With no care for their own safety, Holly, with Pinofita clinging on inside her hood, began to run towards the gully. This time there was no careful crawling through the bushes to enter the gully unseen, Holly just had to get back to the village as soon as possible. When they reached the top of the gully Holly stood still for a moment, silhouetted against the moonlight, to prepare herself for a fast descent of the stony, slippery gully. Off they went slipping and sliding down the slope, Holly using her pole to steady herself and thinking they were making great progress and would soon be back in the village to give the attack plan details to her father.

All was going well as Holly reached the half-way point in the gully, when a large, rough hand shot out from behind a rock and grabbed Holly by the cape.

'Gotcha!' said a cruel voice.

14

A SIGN, ANY SIGN

A T THAT SAME moment back in the village, Boda was moving quickly amongst the children who were huddled together in a scared and nervous group, frantically asking if any of them had seen her daughter. The children who were all very young shook their worried heads, and their concerned faces were lit by the light of several flickering torches making the whole scene more unreal, and more like a bad nightmare to Holly's mother. After two desperate searches amongst the group, she realized Holly was not there, but couldn't think where she could be. In her panic, Boda left the group and ran hurriedly to where Eryk was waiting in the shadow of one of the first houses – where he had thought the attack would be made.

'What are you doing here?' he exclaimed to his wife, 'you need to be keeping Holly safe.'

The tears running down her cheeks that glistened in the torchlight made his heart miss a beat. 'What's wrong?' he asked putting his arm around his wife's shoulders and hugging her to him.

Boda looked up into his concerned face and admitted desperately, 'I can't find Holly anywhere, she is not where she is supposed to be. She ... she's gone!'

Eryk suppressed his own jolt of alarm. He quickly asked her to try and remember when was the last time she had seen their daughter.

'We were all together when we left our home for the gathering. She was with me when you spoke to the villagers to try and agree a plan, then I came to join you and I think that was the last time I remember seeing her.'

They both stood in silence holding one another for comfort when Boda suddenly covered her mouth with a hand and gasped out, 'Oh, oh no! My last sight of Holly was just as you said we needed to know what their plan of attack was! That's where she is, she's gone to find that out. She's in the forest looking for their camp!'

With that Boda put her arms around Eryk and clung to him and cried like she had never done before. Her whole body shook with each gasping breath and tears stained Eryk's cloak.

Eryk held his wife closer than ever, blinking away the wetness which misted his own eyes in the flickering torchlight. Then he bent his head to whisper in her ear, 'I think you're probably right – that's the brave but foolhardy sort of thing she would do, with no thought for her own safety. But we have to remember one very important thing.'

Looking up at him, Boda didn't say a word.

Eryk added quietly, 'Don't forget, she's not alone. She has Pinofita with her and that must count for something mustn't it?'

Slowly Boda nodded her head and, even though her face still showed her terror, within the darkest, deepest depths of her glistening eyes there appeared a tiny inner light, the first flickering spark of hope.

IN THE GULLY, Holly was so shocked and surprised when a hand stretched out of the darkness that she shrieked in fear. As her body was jerked back by the hand's grip, Pinofita fell from her shoulder and became caught in the folds of her rough shirt under the cover of the cloak. He clung on desperately to stop himself from falling to the stony ground.

The rough hand belonged to the hooded scout who had been sent by the warlord to spy on the village. As he was returning with the news about the village reaction to the message delivered by the old man, from the middle of the gully where he was in shadows, he briefly saw a small, cloaked figure appear silhouetted against the moon at the top of the gully. Quickly he had hidden behind a rock, not out of fear but in readiness to catch whoever was coming towards him.

And that's what he had just done!

Holly kicked and screamed in an attempt to break away from his tight grip, but the hooded man was much bigger and stronger than she was so her struggles achieved nothing.

'Stop wriggling about will you, or I'll make you stop,'

snarled his voice in the darkness.

Holly stopped moving, not because she was afraid of the threat but because she felt a small body swaying about wildly clinging on to her shirt somewhere near the middle of her back. Poor Pinofita was not safely in her hood, he was in danger of being knocked to the stony path and trodden on. With that thought, Holly stopped struggling and let her mind concentrate on what to do next.

'Come on,' said the man gruffly, 'get walking back up to the camp.'

Holly looked up into the man's face and put on a scared, little voice.

'Please, I need my stick to help me walk.'

'Why?' the hooded man growled as he looked down at her through dark, evil eyes.

Holly continued in her fake small voice. 'I've twisted my ankle and cut my knee, so have to have my stick to lean on as I walk, look.'

With that Holly pointed to the blood, now dried, on her knee and pretended to hobble as though her right foot had been twisted. The man stared at the little girl before him and believing she was no threat whatsoever, agreed she could have her stick, if that meant she would be quicker getting up the slope to the camp.

Holly picked up her pole and, with the blunt end under her right arm and the pointed end digging into the path, she used it as a crutch to make her way as slowly as possible up the slope, all the time trying to feel with her body where her little friend was.

Finally, with the hooded man's hand on her arm

tugging her along, they cleared the top of the gully, they set out across the flatter grassy ground of the clearing towards the camp fires, the warlord's tent and the small army of hunters. Holly, to her great relief, felt a familiar little weight climb up onto her shoulder and nuzzle into her neck. Pinofita was safe and that gave Holly a sharp rush of hope that whatever came next, she would not be alone, they would face it together.

HOLLY'S FATHER HAD called everyone who could leave their defensive positions to gather together under a few spluttering torches to tell them what he and his wife had discovered. The villagers listened in horror as he explained that they believed Holly – he didn't mention her little brown furry friend – had left the village to go and find out what the leader and the armed men intended to do when attacking the village. Gasps of disbelief came from some the villagers as well as a few voices that said how brave she was to do that for them, maybe silly, but definitely brave.

'Do you want to mount a rescue party?' asked one, volunteering.

Eryk shook his head. Everyone could see that it pained him to do so. 'We would lose our best fighters and lose the village in trying. I think we have to accept that while she is in that camp we cannot help her. But now we keep looking to the gully and the forest above it for any sign that Holly is on her way back and needs our help. Then, as fast as we can run, we will go and bring her home safely.'

He didn't ask for their agreement. He just took Boda's hand and both of them turned to face the moonlit fields, the deep scar of the gully, the dark brooding forest above and, with hearts beating fast, they waited for a sign, any sign.

15

FACING THE WARLORD

THE SCOUT HALF dragged Holly to his leader's tent. Seeing them coming, one of the guards ducked his head closer to the opening and called, 'My lord, our spy is back – the one you sent to the village – and he has a prisoner.'

Immediately, the tent flap opened and out came the warlord dressed in only his shirt, trousers and boots. His thick leather top had been taken off in readiness for bed, as had the belt with the dagger in it. He glared at the small figure before him in a hooded cloak, resting awkwardly on a pole that seemed to be supporting some of her weight. A small girl such as this was no possible threat to him.

All of a sudden, he grabbed her arm and pulled her towards him. He towered over her and when he spoke, leaning down to stare her in the face, the smell of his breath made Holly grimace and shrink back. She couldn't describe the smell, it was just disgusting.

The warlord took this reaction to be fear and, satisfied, he asked, 'Why is someone so small and weak as you out in the forest on your own this late?'

Holly wanted to scream in his face she was not weak, or alone, and had completed her task of finding out his plans to attack her village. And by the way she was only shrinking back because the smell of his breath was horrible.

But she didn't.

Instead, Holly kept up the pretence with a small frightened little voice and replied slowly, 'I ... I was out in the forest picking berries for my mother when I slipped, cut my knee and twisted my ankle. So that's why I need to lean on this stick and, I walk so slowly I couldn't get home before dark, which I would have done had I been able to walk and run at my usual speed.'

The warlord looked at the man who had captured her and raised an eyebrow as a way of asking for some confirmation from him about the truthfulness of what Holly had just said. The man coughed to clear his throat and then agreed that Holly was a slow walker and seemed to need the stick to rest upon and help her walk.

The warlord looked back at Holly with his dark suspicious eyes, 'So where are your berries that you have been picking all day?'

Holly faltered with her answer but replied that when she tripped, she had lost all the berries, and now with a pole to help her walk she couldn't pick any more as she only had one hand free, and she had lost the basket she had used to hold the berries.

Holly wasn't used to lying and the warlord looked down at Holly with a suspicious glare on his dark veined bearded face, until the silence around her grew deeper and more threatening. Most of the other men had now gathered in front of the warlord to witness this interrogation of the strange little girl.

What he said next shocked Holly so much she began to shake.

'You,' bellowed the warlord at close range, 'have no berry juice on your fingers so you're not telling me the truth. I can tell when people lie and you're lying. You're telling me a silly little story to cover your real reason for being out here. But it doesn't matter. You're from the village below the gully and all those villagers will meet their fate tomorrow when I attack, so no need for you to wait until tomorrow to discover your fate is there?!'

He gave her a cruel smile when he had finished speaking and he could feel Holly shaking beneath his grip. He assumed she was so scared that she was paralysed by fear, but far from it. The truth was her shaking was also the result of a rising indignation and anger that grew and grew inside her. She gripped her pole even more tightly and waited for her chance to come when she could finally do something.

The trouble was Holly didn't know what that something might be or when her chance might come.

Looking at the spy who had captured Holly, the warlord spoke to him in a rasping voice. 'You found her – you take care of her. Take her into the forest and leave her there … permanently.'

The man grinned and bowed to his master.

Thinking it was all over and he was done with the fearful, shaking little girl standing in front of him, the warlord let go of Holly's arm in readiness for the man to seize her. He then raised his head and spoke loudly to urge his men to get ready for the attack in the morning. If he had bothered to continue to look Holly in the eye, he would have seen it was far from over, and what the so-called fearful little girl did next took the warlord and all his men completely by surprise.

16

THE SECOND GIFT REVEALED

AS THE WARLORD released Holly's arm and lifted his head to speak, Holly raised her right arm, which was gripping her pole very tightly, and then, with all her strength, she rammed the pointed end into the warlord's left foot.

He screamed with pain and toppled forward with arms outstretched into the spy who had captured Holly and who was at that very moment reaching out to grab Holly to take her into the forest one last time.

The warlord and the spy became entangled, and both stumbled and fell into the rows of other men standing behind them. Then all the men who fell began to try to get up but only they got in each other's way causing them to trip over one another and fall back to the ground again. It was a tangle of arms, legs and bodies, in short it was total chaos and a chorus of shouts, shrieks and angry commands didn't help the situation either. The hunters who were not in the heaving mass on the ground stepped forward to try to help but they couldn't really do anything, such was the knot of arms, legs and heads in front of them.

When all this began to happen a small voice near Holly's ear shouted, *'Run, hide!'*

She did, sprinting across the short distance to the tent, trying to get inside as it was somewhere, anywhere, to hide. Holly had to drop her pole because she needed both hands to pull the heavy flap open. She was in such a hurry to get into the tent and away from the men outside, she didn't pick up her pole before crashing through the flap and into the dimly lit tent. Once in the tent, Holly was stumbling forward so quickly and so off-balance that she was unable to stop herself running into the warlord's low travel bed.

As her legs bashed into the low wooden sides of the bed, she somersaulted head over heels and landed with a thump on the other side. Slightly dazed, Holly sat up and felt the lump of something hard under her leg. Reaching to find out what it was, Holly was surprised to close her hand over the handle of the warlord's dagger.

There were loud shouts outside. Holly knew she had little time to get herself and Pinofita out of the tent and to find somewhere to hide while they gave up searching, and then a way back to their village.

Knowing she couldn't lift the heavy tent edge high enough for her to crawl under, she thought for a moment, smiled grimly, and then drew the dagger from its sheath. Standing close to the back wall of the tent, Holly raised the dagger and thrust it forward in a sharp stabbing motion.

The dagger easily went through the animal skin wall

and, when she pulled down hard on the dagger, the keen blade swiftly cut through the skin leaving a neat slit in the tent wall big enough for Holly to step through. This she did and, still clutching the dagger, she ran as fast as she could over the grassy clearing towards the waiting darkness and the safety of the trees.

Heart racing, she heard the roar behind her when the warlord finally untangled himself from the other struggling men and stood, his face like thunder, and as angry as he had ever been before in his life.

'Where is she?' he yelled, 'which way did she go?'

One man nervously replied, 'Into your tent my lord. She ran into your tent.'

The warlord shouted, 'Men, guard the front of the tent so she doesn't escape and two of you bring me some of the dogs, now. Hurry.'

Holly, still running to the trees, heard the shouted command to get the dogs and shuddered at the thought of what that would have meant for her had she still been in the tent.

A few more strides and Holly reached the safety of the trees where she threw herself onto the ground panting and trying to get her breath back.

'We made it Pinofita,' she panted, 'we made it.'

Holly didn't really notice when Pinofita didn't reply since she was so grateful and relieved to be out of the clutches of the leader of the hooded men, out of the animal skin tent and now within the relative safety of the trees.

The two men sent to get the dogs did so in record time and were now standing with three of the large hounds on leashes by the warlord's side.

'Get ready young lady,' he snarled, staring at the tent with hatred in his eyes, 'time to find out what's in store for your village friends tomorrow.'

He signaled for the men handling the dogs to get ready to release them and raised his arm in readiness to let it fall, the signal to release the dogs. All the other assembled hunters in front of the tent watched with eager eyes and cruel grins.

Back in the trees Holly had regained her breath and asked Pinofita if he was all right after their lucky escape. No answer came. Holly, now slightly concerned, reached into her cape to touch Pinofita and repeated her question. 'Pinofita, are you all right or are you hurt?'

When there was no reply this time, Holly started to panic and hurriedly took her cape off and spread it on the forest floor. Then she knelt and began to check every fold and every nook and cranny of the cape. After half a minute of frantic searching Holly raised her face to the night sky and screamed, 'NO!'

Pinofita was nowhere to be found. He'd gone!

CROUCHING ON THE ground in the corner behind the bed, Pinofita came round to hear the warlord commanding his men to get ready to release the dogs into the tent. When Holly had somersaulted over the bed in the warlord's tent, he had been thrown out of her hood and into one of the dark corners of the tent, where his head had struck the ground very hard making him dazed and confused for a few moments.

Now Pinofita heard the warlord's awful words and realised the dogs were meant to attack and hurt Holly. Pinofita thought of his dear friend and began to get angry at the thought of what might have happened to her had she still been in the tent. He then had the awful thought that, once the dogs found Holly was not in the tent, they would quickly find and follow her scent through the tear in the back wall and track her to wherever she had run. She was not safe from them, unless someone, or something, stopped them.

He stood in the shadows behind the bed and felt himself become so angry that the hair on his body began to rise and his eyes started to feel hot.

If you had had the misfortune to be in that same tent on that very night looking at Pinofita standing in the corner, not only would you have seen every hair on his body bristle with anger, making him look bigger than he was, but you would also have seen his two big black eyes begin to change, from black to two eyes burning like red hot coals blazing in the darkness.

As the warlord dropped his arm, the guard opened the tent flap and the two men holding the dogs released them. The three baying dogs with fangs gleaming in the firelight leapt for the opening.

Once in the dimly lit tent, their initial rush was halted by the fact they could see nothing to attack and ... there was a strange smell.

Not the smell of the single torch that burned low in

its stand impaled into the ground just to their left, nor the smell of the warlord's clothes strewn over the floor. No, it was something else, something coming from the shadows behind the bed.

Having located where the strange smell was coming from, all three dogs faced the bed and, with low, menacing growls, they prepared to attack. But, before they launched themselves at the bed, something happened to make them stop dead in their tracks. It even silenced their growling, as they all stared at a shape that grew and grew in front of them.

A shape they had never seen before, something the size of two of them put together, with sharp claws, two massive front teeth, a tail that lashed from side to side and two red burning eyes.

In his desperation to find a way to save Holly, Pinofita had finally discovered the second secret gift of his visit to the pine tree he had once been a part of.

Out of the dark from behind the bed and into the flickering torchlight of the tent, a truly massive Pinofita launched himself at the three hunting dogs!

What unfolded in the next few minutes was a complete shock to the warlord and his men; they all stopped grinning and, in the moonlight, a shadow started to slowly cross all their cruel faces, a growing shadow of uncertainty and fear.

They had expected to hear the screams of terror from a small girl with a limp, but instead there was an awful deafening roar. On hearing this this loud noise, the warlord shouted, 'It's wolves, they have somehow got into my tent!'

The warlord then realised it wasn't wolves since the roar was made even more frightening by the fact it sounded like a massively deep and loud squeak!

17

THE BLACK AVENGER

IN THE SHADOWS within the trees behind the camp, two ears flapped at the sound of the loud fighting squeak. The huge black bull aurochs felt his heart beat quickening, his breathing becoming faster and, as he lowered his shaggy head with the wide sharp tipped horns, his heavy front hooves pawed the ground beneath them.

Now he knew the answer to the question *'when?'*

It was time!

ALL WAS CHAOS in the tent, with bodies, legs and tails all seemingly tangled into one huge ball of biting teeth, scratching claws and savage snarling and squeaking noises. The dogs had hunted many forest animals before and had always been able to bring their quarry down, but this time was different.

The creature they fought with now was like nothing they had come across before; it was enormous and incredibly strong, with sharp teeth and hair so thick that their bites barely penetrated. It had a tail that it whipped from side to side with such force that it knocked one of them into the air causing it to crash into the torch stand and send the flaming torch into the dry tent wall.

Outside, everyone was watching the sides of the tent bulge as bodies inside crashed against its skin walls, and they listened nervously to the growls, snarls and loud squeaks. They were now sure they were squeaks, impossibly loud ones, but squeaks nevertheless, causing them to grip their spears even tighter.

Then the smallest of the hunting dogs crashed out of the tent flap entrance and, with a howl of despair, raced between the rows of armed men and into the blackness of the forest. One of the tent walls began to glow from the inside, as the torch flames took hold and licked higher up the dry skin wall.

The warlord had finally had enough. Something strange was fighting his dogs and now his precious animal skin tent was in danger of being destroyed. He rallied his hunters with shouts for some of them to put out the fire and for all the others to take their sharp spears and follow him into the tent to deal with whatever it was in there. That meant nearly twenty spears were soon going to be added to the two remaining dogs that Pinofita still faced – too many to beat, even for him.

But a few of the armed men looked at one another with a real growing look of fear on their faces. One of them said, 'What, go into a burning tent to face some strange monster of the forest that can fight three of the dogs on its own?'

As the rest of the men took a hesitant step forward to follow their master, the man who had just spoken turned and ran the other way.

He didn't get far before he stopped running and, with his eyes bulging out of his head with disbelief, he screamed a blood-curdling cry of total fear that echoed around the clearing and bounced off the forest edge tree walls.

Every one of the hunters and the warlord stopped in mid-step and turned.

What they saw in the moonlight made their blood run cold.

Charging down from the forest, the noise of his cloven hooves muffled by the grass, was the massive black bull aurochs.

Neither the growing fire in the tent nor the various camp fires deterred the beast. The large group of men with spears did not cause him to falter either. This was his destiny and he raced forward with only one thought running through his whole, huge body. Revenge. Revenge for all the destruction he had seen these men do over the years.

Just a few moments after the scream rent the night, the hunter who had been running towards him was flattened to the ground with a sickening crunch.

The bull didn't even notice. He continued with his headlong charge. Without caring about the spears ahead of him, the aurochs crashed into the waiting crowd. Most had no time to flee before the sharp horns and heavy hooves began to wreak havoc amongst them.

The warlord was not among the struggling mass of screaming bodies being tossed and trampled by the black shadow. He had been behind his group of men and, in the few extra seconds he had to react, he threw himself to one side of the burning tent out of sight.

From within the tent, the two remaining dogs raced out into the chaos. They couldn't bring their quarry down and the flames on one side of the tent scared them just as much as the teeth and claws facing them. Outside was no better. In desperation, they took one look at the aurochs and did what defeated, frightened creatures do. They ran away into the night, howling as they went.

A great lunge of the aurochs' head caught the tent side with a sharp tipped horn. He felt the resistance and believed the men were holding him in some way. He fought to free himself and tossed his great head as high and as far to the side as he could. No skin tent could resist such brutal force. With a great tearing sound, it fell in tatters and the flames grew in ferocity.

Feeling the force holding his head give way, the aurochs was even more determined to complete the task he had been given, and to fight with the last of his strength any foe who was still standing before him.

As he turned, he found himself facing twelve rather shaken hooded men who stood holding their wavering spears out in front of them. However, instead of charging as the hunters feared he would, he stood very still and just stared at them, letting his heartbeat slow down and his breathing become deeper and easier. It was as though he knew they were defeated and would no longer pose a threat to the forest and the animals in it.

Several long seconds passed, while the hands holding the spears trembled. Then, at last, the huge black bull turned away and without a second glance, he ambled off towards the forest with only a few cuts and scratches to show from his fight.

As his black bulk began to merge with the dark forest, the calming hand he had felt resting lightly on his forehead as he ripped his horn clear from the tent now lifted and melted away. His task was complete.

18

A SIGN

THE HUNTERS COULD not understand what had just happened. First some creature that squeaked had been fighting three dogs in the tent, then a massive black aurochs had appeared from nowhere, and now it had just turned and returned to the forest as though nothing had happened. Plus, and this worried them the most, they could no longer see their warlord master.

Without his commanding voice and presence to hold them together, several of the hunters panicked and, picking up their spears, ran into the forest in the general direction of their castle home. The remaining hooded men just stood and watched their companions flee, unsure of what to do next.

Then something moved in the flaming ruins of the tent.

Someone made a small sound of terror. They all stood transfixed as a figure rose from under the fallen tent skins. They held their breath and wondered if this was the strange creature that had fought with the dogs moments before. They were almost at the point of running away when the figure shouted.

'Where are you all?'

After a moment's pause the familiar voice continued, 'Gather round me now and prepare to attack whatever was attacking my dogs, for it must show itself now the tent has collapsed and is on fire.'

It was their master, looking very shaken and not his usual strong self. Once the warlord had managed to break free from the burning tent, his men gathered around him and readied their weapons.

But before anyone could do or say anything else the burning tent unexpectedly whooshed with a high plume of flames. Soon there was nothing left but ash and charred wood. Of Pinofita, there was no sign.

DOWN IN THE village the watching group saw the glow of the fire. Then a plume of flames shot into the night sky.

'That's it!' shouted Holly's parents. 'The sign we have been waiting for.'

Holly's father gripped his axe and his burning torch and began to head for the gully at a fast run, followed by the strongest of the armed villagers carrying their weapons and flaming torches. They ran across the fields and towards the dark gully, which they began to climb as fast as they could.

BLIND WITH RAGE and grief, Holly ran as fast as she could back towards the burning camp. She had seen the tent collapse. She knew it would be impossible for any brave mouse to survive that, even Pinofita, but now the warlord's men were closing in and if her beloved friend was caught by them … she didn't know what she would be able to do, but she had to try.

She lifted the stolen dagger in her hand. As she reached about halfway she had to dodge past a dog-sized rock she could have sworn wasn't there when she ran from the tent. With no time to think about obstacles in her path for more than for a fleeting second, Holly focused her mind on what she needed to do in the hope she could find and save her little furry friend.

In the next split second, Holly tripped over what she assumed was a root sticking up out of the ground and was falling forwards into the grass. She fell with a crash. The dagger flew from her grip.

Holly was slightly dazed but determination made her sit up ready to get to her feet and resume her charge on the enemy camp. But then a tiny, warm, furry body jumped onto her arm and then less than a second later, nuzzled into her neck.

'Pinofita!'

Holly's eyes filled with tears, not of despair and grief, but of pure joy. She cuddled her friend and wept. 'Where were you? Were you trapped in the tent? Did you see what was fighting the dogs? How did you escape?'

'We can't stay here out in the open, Holly,' said Pinofita in the gentlest voice he had, 'we need to get to the trees before we are discovered.'

Holly sniffed, wiped her eyes and nose on her sleeve and clambered to her feet ready to go back to the safety of the trees, when a loud angry voice shouted.

'There, over there, she's out there in the clearing!'

Startled and suddenly afraid, Holly looked back over her shoulder and saw the leader of the hunters standing by the still blazing tent and pointing directly in her direction.

'Come on men,' called the cruel and angry warlord, 'we have her in the open, come on let's get her.'

The warlord ran forward, but not as quickly as Holly. Clutching Pinofita, she ran from him and just before he reached the spot where Holly had been standing, his foot trod on something hard. He stopped, looked down into the grass and a savage glint returned to his cruel eyes. His dagger. The girl must have taken it from his bedside in the tent before it burnt down. Whilst stooping to pick up his dagger he turned to see where his men were, as they had yet to catch up with him despite his loud command to do so.

What he saw when he turned made him catch his breath and his stomach crawl with a new fear.

For beyond his men, from the direction of the village, he could see flaming torches appearing over the top of the gully.

19

TORCHES IN
THE NIGHT

ERYK AND HIS small team of the best fighters from the village entered the clearing and advanced to where the warlord's now ruined camp was smoking in the night air. Holly's father didn't know how many armed men they were about to face, nor did he care. He was here to save his brave daughter.

The warlord ran back to his remaining men. They were all standing motionless looking in horror at the approaching torches. The hunters were not expecting to be attacked; they were the ones who were going to do the attacking but, after the recent events with the small girl, the creature in the tent and then the chaos caused by the black aurochs, they were feeling rather shaken. They couldn't see who, or what, was carrying the torches this time, but they continued to just stare and do nothing, rooted to the spot by uncertainty and growing fear, a fear that painted itself across each and every one of their faces.

The warlord screamed at them. 'Don't just wait to

be attacked, attack them. Look at how many torches there are, there aren't many of them so come on, charge and defeat them. Then we win these woodlands and our rightful hunting. Do it now – attack!'

Halfheartedly, the hunters gathered themselves to charge the line of torches. The bravest of them began to move forwards. Then they suddenly stopped. More lights appeared over the top of the gully – more torches, lots of them.

The men and the warlord hesitated as there were now so many more torches than before and, assuming one villager held one torch, there must have been three or four times as many people facing them than they numbered themselves.

The hooded men stepped back and the warlord, who couldn't understand where all these extra defenders had come from, realised it was pointless to attack. He was defeated.

What he had to do now was to avoid capture – or worse – and so he uttered a command he never thought he would. He raised his dark bearded head high and yelled into the night sky as loud as he could.

'Fall back men, retreat, run for your lives!'

The once confident hunters needed no second order to tell them to flee. As one, including the warlord, they turned and, carrying what weapons they had, they collected the remaining dogs, and then they ran as fast as their legs would take them back across the clearing and into the forest.

20

A SHAPE IN
THE SMOKE

ALL THE FIGHTERS from the village cheered to see the armed men turn and run but didn't understand how so few of them had made them run away like cowards without putting up some sort of fight.

When Eryk turned, he saw what the warlord had seen, an impossible number of torches coming towards them from the top of the gully. As the throng of torches came closer, he could see who was actually carrying them.

Not some large army but the brave people who had been left behind in the village – the old folk, the children and the untrained men and women, all carrying two flaming torches each held high in the night sky.

Boda ran forward from the group of women and children she had led from the village and, after handing her torches to two of the men who stood either side of Eryk, she fell into his arms and hugged him with all her might.

'They've gone haven't they? We're safe from the horrible threat of the warlord!'

Eryk took a moment to send two of the villagers after the warlord, to track them as they fled incase they doubled back again. Then he added to his wife, 'Now we just need to find Holly.'

'Where is she?' gasped Boda, 'haven't you seen her yet?'

'No, not yet,' said her husband, turning to cast his gaze over the smouldering camp, 'but she must be here. Someone's responsible for all this,' and under his breath so no one else could hear except his wife, he added, 'and it can't have been her tiny, furry friend!'

The villagers now all spread out in a line across the clearing and, with their torches held high, began to walk slowly towards the dying embers of the camp where the plume of smoke was now blowing sideways in the slight breeze. They called out Holly's name so, if she were close and could hear them, she would know she was safe from harm.

Walking forward slowly, the line of villagers suddenly halted, for coming towards them, a small shape was beginning to materialise within the smoke. The reaction of some of the villagers was to run, not knowing what on earth this shape might be, and they had all heard stories about strange things that lived in these woods.

One person who did run was Boda, but she ran towards, not away from the strange shape in the smoke. With a loud shout of, 'Holly!' Boda ran excitedly to meet her daughter. Both were crying tears of relief and joy when they ran full tilt into one another's arms.

As they hugged each other, the night was filled with the sound of happy villagers all waving their torches aloft, celebrating their escape from a terrible fate, and chanting, 'Holly, Holly, Holly!'

21

A SORE SPOT

IT WAS ALMOST time for the sun to appear in the eastern sky by the time Holly was safely tucked up in bed with Pinofita curled up on her pillow. She had recounted her full adventure; the climb up the gully, the awful plan she had overheard which would have destroyed the village, and her escape into the trees after stabbing the warlord in the foot with her pole. She even described the horror of leaving Pinofita behind in the tent and the sight of it collapsing into flames, and her desperation to go back to save her little furry friend. Pinofita stayed very quiet.

As her parents lay next to each other in their bed, Holly's father said slowly, 'I still don't get it. Why would the dogs fight amongst themselves in the tent, and if Holly didn't start that fire, what caused the chaos we saw in the camp?'

Boda didn't reply. She just breathed gently and evenly in her exhausted sleep next to him.

Up in the rafters, Holly snuggled down in her cozy bed with her tired head on her soft pillow and, with

Pinofita in his usual place by her neck, she murmured, 'How *did* you get out of the tent?'

Pinofita paused before he replied. In his mind was the memory of growing to a monstrous size while fighting the dogs and then realising that there were lots of armed men who could enter the tent with their spears and swords at any moment. He remembered being trapped by the fire, and how, in the last moment before things became truly hopeless, the whole tent shuddered and then began to rise at one end as the animal skins were ripped apart.

Things then started to happen very quickly. Distracted from his fight, Pinofita unconsciously began to shrink slowly back to his normal size. He climbed through the tear in the tent that Holly had made and, on reaching the grass outside, began to run towards the trees, guessing Holly would have done the same. Within less than half a minute of him escaping from the tent, the whole structure inexplicably lifted and then disintegrated into a shower of red and yellow flames.

Pinofita didn't know how to explain what had happened when he had fought the dogs, or what had happened to stop the warlord's men from charging into the tent. So he simply said, 'The tent collapsed and I was able to climb out. I was nearly halfway to the trees when I saw something truly terrifying.'

'You did? What was it?'

'It wasn't the sound of the warlord shouting orders to find the strange creature in the ruins of the tent, it was the sight of a certain young girl racing towards me, towards the blazing tent and the camp full of hunters, with a dagger held high in her hand and no regard whatsoever for her own safety!'

He didn't mention that by that time he had shrunk to about the size of a hunting dog.

Holly smiled in the dark. 'Do you remember a rock and a tree root in the clearing where we found each other?'

A little voice replied, 'No, I don't think so but it was dark and scary so we could easily have missed it.'

After a short pause, Pinofita heard his brave friend reply, 'I guess you're right. Night night Pinofita.'

'Night night Holly,' said her little friend, who didn't go to sleep until he had rubbed better the sore spot on his tail where Holly had kicked it when she tripped over it!

22

THE SECRET CAVITY

OUT IN THE forests to the north, the warlord and his band of hunters, who now numbered a lot fewer than when they had set out, slowly made their way home to the castle in the blackened clearing. After three long days and nights slowly travelling north having nothing to eat but berries, roots and only water from streams to drink, they finally reached the safety of the castle with its high wooden outer stockade and the cold stone buildings within.

Now the warlord was sitting in his throne-like chair by a roaring fire in his great hall in the stone castle tower.

For the first time in a long time, he felt angry – truly angry at the defeat he had suffered over the events of the last few days, especially when he considered the part played by the small girl with a limp who had been captured near his camp. His foot still hurt from the sharp pole she had stabbed into it and the long trek home had made it throb even more.

He was angry and he wanted revenge on the village, but more so he wanted revenge on the little girl who had ruined all his plans. For over an hour he brooded. His armed men were now so few, and even his pack of hunting dogs was down to just two. He needed something to turn things to his favour and to rid him of the villagers, especially that girl.

He thought some more then, with a great sigh, he rose out of his chair and walked with a slight limp towards the stone wall at the back of the great hall.

A decision had been made.

When the warlord stood in front of the middle of the wall, he moved his dark veined hand over the stones as though he was counting them. Four down, then five to the right and finally one stone up. Removing a cleverly concealed loose stone from the wall revealed a dark secret cavity. With a strange look of uncertainty on his face, he reached into the black space and retrieved a crystal jar sealed by a wood and leather stopper.

The warlord limped slowly back to his chair carrying the crystal container carefully in both hands. Once comfortably seated, he cradled it as if unsure, or just apprehensive. Then he held it away from his body and holding it with both hands, he shook it.

A reddish swirling mist appeared within the depths of the jar and words in gold began to form and glisten on its sides in the firelight. As the red mist grew brighter, so too did the golden message. The warlord read the familiar words …

One wish but be careful what you wish for

His dark veined fingers rested motionlessly on the

sealed top and then they began tapping the wood and leather stopper. With a grunt of effort and a final grimace of determination on his dark-veined face, his gnarled fingers gripped and gave a twist. The seal was broken!

Outside the castle the vast moonlit forest was silent except for an occasional owl call. Then, as if on a command, a deathly silence fell upon the forest. After a few moments of unearthly quiet the moonlit silence was broken by the long drawn-out howl of a wolf that echoed through the trees. A howl that was a warning to some who heard it, and for others, the sound of hope.

PART 2

OUT OF THE LIGHT

23

PIECES OF THE JIGSAW

HOLLY'S FATHER AND his friends were looking carefully at the clearing at the top of the gully where they had confronted the hooded men and watched them run away. There were the remains of the camp fires and the larger area of ash where the tent had burned to the ground but, in front of where the tent would have stood, the ground was churned up and the men could see nothing but a trampled area of blood-stained grass, mud and broken spears.

They hadn't fought with the armed men so why was there blood? They were busy collecting the spears when one of the villagers called out from a place a bit further away from the camp fire remains and nearer the forest edge. He called to them, but his head didn't turn, he just stood staring at the ground and pointing with his right hand at something in the grass.

They all ran to him and looked at where he was pointing. In the grass was a small patch of softer ground and, within this, clear as day for anyone to see, was a huge cloven hoof print deeply impressed into the ground.

They all stared and then, without a sound, looked at one another. Their faces seemed to ask one another, what on earth made that?

The older man standing next to Eryk spoke first, his voice quiet and slightly wondrous. 'It's been ages since I last saw a print like that and I know what animal made it.'

'What did it?' chorused his friends.

The man smiled a grim smile and, with a tinge of fear in his voice, he replied, 'Aurochs, and being that size of hoof print it must be a huge one at that!'

All the men studied the hoof print with a certain reverence and then they all looked up and stared around nervously at the silent forest that surrounded them, just in case it was still close.

'So,' said Holly's father, 'an aurochs bull then?'

The older man nodded in agreement. Eryk continued to question him further.

'Would that animal have been strong enough to devastate the warlord's army?'

The older man again nodded. He couldn't trust his voice to speak in a normal way. If he had spoken, his voice would have betrayed to his friends how afraid he was.

Holly's father asked no more questions, but he was deep in thought and, the more he thought, the more pieces of the story he had heard from Holly fell into place. As he and the other foresters returned to their work in the forest, Eryk kept turning the events of that night over in his mind. He now knew all the chaos outside the tent and the disarray among the warlord's men was

126

because of the aurochs bull.

However, that still didn't explain the dogfight Holly had described. Had another creature of the forest been inside the tent? If so, it had left no trace or sign of its presence.

What sort of creature could do that, he wondered? There had to be an explanation, another reason, but what? No matter how hard he thought about it, he could not make sense of everything his daughter had described.

FOR HOLLY AND Pinofita, it was like nothing had ever happened. They were once again exploring the forest. The two villagers who had been sent after the retreating warlord had returned and declared that all was now well, and the danger had passed. Boda said it was best to get things back to normal, and for Holly and Pinofita, that meant being in the woods.

The forest was alive with the sound of birdsong and Holly, with Pinofita snugly cuddled into her neck, walked happily though the trees and glades seeing more of the forest creatures than ever before. The animals and birds had all understood Pinofita's message that Holly was to be trusted; she was one of them and as one with the green woods and that made her special, very special indeed.

24

ONCE A GOOD MAN

WHEN THE WARLORD was a much younger man, he was honest and good, someone you would trust. So trusted that his chieftain had made him his warlord over the small band of six dedicated warriors who, under his command, sought out evil in the woodlands and mountains where they lived to try and make it a better place for ordinary village folk to live.

They had been together as a band of warriors for several years when they faced their hardest and most dangerous task. Villages in the west of their chieftain's realm were being terrorized by a cruel witch who brought pain and suffering to the people. This witch was so powerful she could change her shape very quickly and that made it especially hard for the warriors hunting her to find and catch her. They never knew what she might look like, so they never knew what they were hunting!

But several travellers brought stories about a small village further west, where the families living there had been attacked by the witch, or where she had even made people disappear. The young warlord and his men knew they would have to go to the cursed village and start their search there.

If you had seen that village you would have said it looked normal except, on closer inspection you would have seen that almost everyone stayed inside their homes and no children played outside. People were too scared.

On approaching the village, the warriors met an elderly woman coming towards them carrying a large bundle on her back. The young warlord spoke kindly to the woman and asked why she was out on her own and not safe at home in her village. With a sad look in her eyes, the woman told him she was leaving the village while she could. Her husband had gone missing and so had her young daughter, who was due to be married in the coming summer to a young man from another village. But now that wasn't going to happen. She had packed up what she could carry and she was leaving to go somewhere else. Her main regret, she said, was that her favourite chair – made for her by her husband with acorns carved on the ends of the two arms – was too heavy for her to carry, so sadly, she had had to leave it behind.

Bidding the elderly woman a safe journey, the warriors carried on until they reached the desolate village. It was nearly dark when they arrived, but very few lights were lit in the gloomy houses, and so the young warlord knocked on the first door they came to in the hope they could be shown where they might rest and sleep for the night. The door was partially opened by a nervous young woman, who stared at the warriors on her doorstep, with wide frightened eyes.

'Please don't be afraid,' said the young warlord, 'we are here to help you and all folk of this village, to rid you of a cruel witch we believe is terrorising you.'

The young woman's head nodded and, her bright blue eyes showed real fear and, with a hesitant voice, said she couldn't offer them room in the house but all the men would be welcome to rest for the night in the small barn, if they wanted to.

Gladly the young warlord accepted the kind offer, and the young woman seemed grateful for the protection the warrior group would provide through the long night. The young warlord thanked the woman again, then he and his men walked to the small barn and organised themselves to settle down for the night. They carried very meagre rations, just some dry oatcakes and honey. It wasn't much but it was nourishing and, importantly, light to carry.

As they were beginning their simple supper there was a gentle knock on the barn door. One of the men rose to open it and before him stood the young woman they had just spoken to, carrying six wooden spoons and a large cooking pot. The man's stomach rumbled when he smelled the stew for he was really hungry and it did smell so delicious.

The young woman smiled at the soldier who had opened the door. Holding his attention with her bright blue eyes, she asked gently, 'Would you and the other soldiers like some supper?'

Before he could reply, a chorus of 'Yes!' came from all the warriors as they put their oatcakes and honey to one side and came forward to thank the young woman and to take the spoons and pot from her. As she left, the men put the cooking pot in the centre of the barn floor and sat in a circle around the pot handing the spoons out among the seated group. There were seven warriors, including the young warlord, but only six spoons.

'Don't worry,' laughed the young warlord, 'you eat first then I'll have my turn, just don't eat it all!'

The six soldiers began to dip their spoons into the stew and, after tasting the first mouthful, declared it to be delicious and that the young woman had a rare talent if she could prepare food this good. The young warlord, from his uncomfortable sitting position on the barn floor, saw a partially covered object just behind the man opposite him. He could see ends of what looked like wooden furniture legs but couldn't be sure. He rose and moved to inspect things closer. Pulling the cloth off the object, he revealed what looked in the half-light of the barn to be an old chair.

He thought that would be far more comfortable than the floor, so he pulled the chair into the circle of men and sat down on it. He smiled at the sight of his brave men laughing and tucking into what was a most unexpected and tasty supper. Stretching his tired body out as he sat on the chair, his hands ran down the chair arms and gripped the ends. His fingers found a pleasing carved end to each of the arms, and he gently gripped the strange shapes while his mind automatically tried to tell him what the shapes were that he was feeling.

Finally, his brain registered the shape, ACORNS!

'Stop eating the stew, put the spoons down NOW!'

he shouted

It was too late. All his six men looked at him through sleep-laden eyes as they slumped sideways, backwards or forwards in a dead sleep.

He now knew his men were under a sleeping spell and no use whatsoever for fighting and, worse still, he also knew the kind young woman with the bright blue eyes, who had offered them shelter and supper, was no other than the person they sought – the witch.

He flew out of the chair and quickly drew his sharp sword hoping no other magic would overtake him that night. Quickly he went to the barn door and listened. It was a good thing he had waited because he could hear soft footsteps coming towards the barn. With bated breath he stood ready behind the door and, when it slowly creaked open, he threw himself at the wooden planks of the door with all his might. There was a loud thud as the door slammed into whoever, or whatever, stood just on the other side, followed by a startled scream. Not the scream of a young woman, but the rasping, hollow scream of an old, old woman.

The young warlord with sword in hand quickly stepped through the open door to face what he knew would be waiting for him, an embodiment of evil in whatever form it had taken. Sitting on the ground with a gash across her forehead where the door had hit her sat the witch. Not the young woman who had spoken to the soldiers before, but now a strange figure dressed in long black robes and with straggly thin hair, creased and cracked skin and – this was the scariest thing – blood running down from the cut in her forehead. But the blood wasn't red, it was black!

Her dark crazed eyes glared up at the young warlord but, before she could gather herself, he struck again, this time with his sharp sword. The sword pierced the left side of the chest of the old hag, where her heart should have been but, as you probably know, witches don't have hearts, so the blow wasn't a fatal one; it just made her angrier still.

The only way to kill a witch is to cut her head off. The young warlord remembered this, so prepared to attack again.

As he withdrew his sword to strike a second time, the witch screamed and launched herself at him, arms outstretched with bony hands and talon-like nails. The young warlord was now ready to fight. She leapt up cat-like at him, so he allowed himself to fall backwards out of the reach of her talon-like finger nails, but leaving the point of his sword high. As he fell, and the witches hurtling body shut out the moonlight from his view, he felt his sword connect. Then he hit the ground, and the witch, screaming her pain and anger, span away and crashed through the door of the cottage, the door he had knocked on not so long ago.

He scrambled quickly to his feet and ran into the cottage intent on completing his task of finishing off the witch, only to be faced with the witch crumpled in a heap on the stone flagged floor, holding her neck from which dark black blood gushed. He stopped and stared because instead of an old hag facing him, he was now looking into the bright blue and pained eyes of the young woman.

So shocked was he that he never considered delivering the final fatal sword cut that would sever the witch's head completely from her body. He stood motionless, his sword hanging by his side and waited.

Through her pain, the young woman spoke to him. In a weak and trembling voice, she said, 'You, kind sir, are a good and honest man, and your sword has cleansed the power of the evil witch who stole my body. I am cut and bleeding, but it will heal given time. Will you please give me that time?'

Again, the young warlord hesitated, could this be true he asked himself? Above all else he didn't want to hurt an innocent young woman who had been under the spell of the witch and so his mind became confused as to what to do next.

The young woman continued to speak from the stone flagged floor. 'I know in your heart you are a good man, and I will promise you this. Let me stand before you so you can see my true self and, no matter what you think of me, be assured I will change and with that change you will have anything you wish for.'

Confused by these words the young warlord, who so wanted the witch gone and this young woman to live, as well as wondering how he could have anything he wanted, sheathed his sword. Then with his left hand, he reached out to the young woman to help her rise from the stone flags.

His eyes were strangely fixed on the young woman's bright blue eyes, it was as though he couldn't look away even if he wanted to. As his hand reached out for hers, what happened then changed his life forever and for the worse.

Instead of reaching out to hold his hand, the slender hand of the young woman rapidly changed into the claw-like fingers of the old witch. A blood-soaked talon scratched the young warlord's outstretched hand, allowing a drop of black blood to flow from the nail into the open flesh of his hand. He didn't notice this but, what he did see, was the youthful face and body of the young woman change before his very gaze. The black clothes and the body beneath them began to lose their shape, almost like they were melting in front of his very eyes. However, the melting action didn't change the solid body to a liquid form. Instead the body began to swirl like a heavy mist, a heavy, black mist.

In horror the young warlord watched helplessly as the dark, evil mist began to float and swirl before his eyes, and the old witch's face appeared one last time through the mist. Her now strangled and hollow voice urged him to follow her if he wanted his one wish, for anything in the world he desired!

As he watched, unable to move, the mist turned from black to a blood red, and then began to sink towards the wide cracks between the cold flagstones of the floor. When the swirling red mist reached the crack below it, it slowly and sinuously sank out of sight. After every trace of it had disappeared, the young warlord seemed to come out of his trance, and he could only remember the voice urging him to follow to gain his one wish.

Taking his sword, he pushed the point into the crack between the flagstones and prised one of them up so he could grasp its edge and pull it to one side. As he gripped the edge of the stone and lifted it, he noticed, for the first time, the scratch on his left hand and the deep dark veining now spreading out from the cut, down his hand and up his arm. As the dark veining expanded, his good and honest soul began to shrink and, in its place a darker, crueller nature took hold. He was becoming different.

A cavity was revealed beneath the flagstone. In the darkness of the earthen space, he could see two objects side by side. A crystal jar, within which the blood red mist swirled and pulsed like a living organism and, next to it, a wood and leather stopper that looked like it would fit into the top of the vessel so sealing it tight.

Quickly he took the jar in one hand and the stopper in the other then, holding them firmly he pushed the stopper into the neck of the jar. It fitted perfectly.

Once the stopper was in place, the crystal vessel looked black and cold. Curious as to where the red mist had gone, the warlord took the jar in both hands and, holding it in front of his dark veined neck and face, he shook it. As he did, the red mist swirled within the jar and golden words etched into the side of it appeared.

One wish but be careful what you wish for

That was the signal for the young warlord to forget his old loyalties and his old friends, he wanted that wish, whatever he decided it would be.

So, leaving the small cottage, he put the jar in his leather tunic top and, with his sword sheathed, he left his men in their deep sleep in the barn and, without a backwards glance, he set off towards the vast forest far away to the west.

He had heard about the forest from different travellers but had never visited it. In his darkening mind he decided to find a place where he could settle, away from other people and live the life he was now beginning to imagine for himself, a selfish and cruel life where he would think not of others but only of himself.

25

EVIL COMES TO LIFE

HOLLY AND HER parents were again going over the events of the other night. Holly's mother didn't really want to relive the horror of realising that her daughter had disappeared as it upset her so much but, apparently her husband had some new information, something he said they would find very interesting.

He began by asking his daughter, 'Did you see a bull attack the warlord's camp? An aurochs?'

The blank faces in front of him, from both Holly and Pinofita, answered his question.

Holly said questioningly, 'And what is an aurochs please?'

Before her father could answer Boda cut in quickly. 'This is an old folk story of the forest, an aurochs is supposedly a type of forest bull, but nobody I know has seen one and, as far as I am concerned, they have never been seen in these woods.'

'Really!' exclaimed Holly, 'then why does Father think one attacked the warlord's camp?'

'Because,' said Eryk quietly, 'you told us yourself

– you didn't cause all that destruction, and Pinofita is very small so we don't think he did, and I have seen a hoof print in the soft ground in the clearing. It was an aurochs bull that fought those men on the night before we arrived."

'But why would it do that?' asked Boda.

'I've no idea,' said Eryk, 'Unless …'

'Unless what?' prompted Holly, looking excitedly into her father's eyes.

'Don't say it,' said Boda to her husband with a warning tone in her voice.

'Oh please!' implored Holly, 'unless what?'

Her father looked very seriously at her and said in his most gentle and mysterious voice, 'Unless, as the legend says, the woodland came to our rescue and somehow sent a forest creature to help.'

'Don't listen to him.' Boda laughed gently. 'Since when and how can a forest come to our rescue? We don't speak their many animal languages, if they have any, and the animals and birds certainly don't speak our language.'

Pinofita was sitting in his usual place on Holly's shoulder and looking at Holly's mother and father through all the conversation with his big bright black eyes and his ears wiggling. On hearing what Holly's mother had just said, he wriggled his bottom a little and his whiskers twitched and only Holly heard the tiny voice near her ear mutter. 'Huh, if only they knew!'

'Did you see any other large creatures?' asked her father, 'Anything to explain what happened in the tent to stop the dogs from following you after you fled from the camp?'

Holly's face looked genuinely blank, as she was certain that if a wild forest creature had been in the tent and large enough to fight off three hunting dogs, she would have seen it when she had entered the tent. Holly thought about it some more and slowly a strange idea came to her and slowly grew in her mind, but she dismissed it as just a silly thought.

The silly idea she'd had had been that the only other creature in the tent with her had been Pinofita, but what on earth could Pinofita have done against three hunting dogs? What indeed!

Before the conversation went any further, Holly's mother called an end to it and, with goodnight kisses completed, Holly and Pinofita climbed the rickety ladder up to her tiny room in the cottage roof space. As usual, before jumping into bed, Holly and Pinofita went to the window opening and looked up at the sky with the moon hanging in the dark velvety summer night sky. It looked perfectly normal, as usual, so the two of them sat quietly together looking at it and the bright sparkling stars in the night sky all around. It was another perfect night

IN THE GREAT hall of the castle, seated by the fire in his large chair, the warlord's dark veined fingers rested motionlessly on the wood and leather seal. With a grunt of effort and a final grimace of determination, his gnarled

fingers twisted the stopper.

The seal was broken! The warlord tossed the wood and leather stopper into the fire. Immediately, the flames to burst into greater life, growing and licking higher up the stone chimney.

Holding the jar in both his gnarled hands, the warlord watched and waited, not realising he had forgotten to breathe such was his anticipation of what was to happen. The truth was he had no idea what would happen next but, he believed in one thing; by not severing her head from her body, he had spared the life of the cruel witch. He also remembered she had promised to do two things if he held back from killing her. The first promise was that she would change and, whilst the change he witnessed of the body changing from a human form to a swirling mist was not the change he thought she meant, it was still a change.

He had expected her to change from her evil ways to a kindlier way of life but that obviously was not her plan. But the fact remained that she hadn't lied to him. The second promise made in return for her life was the promise of anything he desired, anything!

The crystal glowed brighter still, like the brightest blood that had ever flowed from a wound. The red mist slowly swirled up out of the vessel and increased in size with each second that passed. The warlord instinctively held the jar further away from his body but kept a firm hold of it as the swirling red mist grew and grew before his widening eyes.

When the cloud of mist was floating in the air above the mouth of the jar and was about the size of a small woman it began to spin, causing bright spots of red light to appear within the depths of the spinning mass. The gyrating slowed and the red mist coalesced into a firmer shape, the shape of a caped hooded woman with long sleeves that covered her arms, if she had any, but no legs only a tapering plume of mist that curled and swayed like a serpent's tail above the ground.

The strange thing was, when the warlord looked at the hood, where the face should have been, all he saw was a deep dark recess going from red to the densest black ever, but no face. Equally strange was that the shape was impossible to focus on; wherever he looked it became almost transparent, except for the deep black hollow of the faceless centre of the hood. So taken aback was the warlord that when he finally breathed again with a loud intake of air, it sounded more like a gasp of growing fear than just a normal breath.

As he sat still clutching the crystal jar, the floating red shape in front of him became very still, then his blood chilled as he heard an old, cracked and hollow voice come from the deep black recess of the hood.

'Aaaaahhhh!! So long in the dark but now almost free.'

The warlord was slightly shocked at the ancient and strange voice but almost instantly he recognised it; it was the voice of the witch he had nearly slain so long ago.

With a growing mixture of revulsion and elation he watched and waited.

The swirling, translucent body, if you could call it a body, was undoubtedly some type of evil spirit, an essence of the witch. He began to feel far better than he had done ever since returning from that humiliating retreat from the clearing when the villagers had arrived to attack him.

The ancient hollow voice broke the silence. 'What is your one wish, my lord?'

Across the great hall, the silence grew again with only the crackle of the logs burning steadily in the hearth to break it. The warlord relished hearing those words from the evil spirit and sat back comfortably to consider what his one wish would be. Words ran amok in his dark mind – words such as 'power, gold, an army, youth.'

In truth, he knew exactly what his wish would be. Taking a deep breath, the warlord looked into the dark recess of the hood and commanded.

'Rid me of the villagers who defeated me in the clearing and especially that wretch of a girl.'

Instead of immediately agreeing to do his bidding the evil spirit replied in her hollow voice, 'That is two wishes my lord, and you only have one, decide.'

Taken aback, the warlord sat silently for a few moments thinking about what the evil one had just said and finally understood why it was two, not one wish. He scowled, thoughts racing through his mind as to what he really wanted, and finally he shouted out so loudly that it echoed all around the great hall and to where his remaining men sat at the long table in the other room.

'Rid me of the girl!'

Almost immediately the door to the great hall burst open and two of the hooded men crashed into the room, thinking the shout they had heard was in fact a command to them. As soon as they entered the room, they saw the

143

red evil spirit floating in front of their master and their stomachs turned over with fear and their knees turned to jelly.

'Stand still,' the warlord ordered them, 'stand still and look carefully at the thing that will finally bring destruction to our enemies.'

The men stood in awe of the evil spirit, heads hung down, so they didn't have to look at it, and both had beads of sweat on their faces created by the fear they felt.

'Go and tell the other men that my command is for you all to stay inside and wait for further instructions, but it would be wise to sharpen your weapons,' the warlord added with an evil grin.

The men hurriedly retreated from the great hall to carry the strange and scary news about the new unearthly weapon the warlord had somehow found. They didn't understand what was going to happen but, if it brought about the defeat of their enemies, they would be happy especially so if they didn't have to face an angry aurochs again.

Once the men had gone, the warlord looked at the swirling form before him and said, 'So, is my one wish clear enough for you now?'

The evil spirit seemed to nod or bow her hooded head, where it would have been had she had one, and then she floated up to the ceiling rafters of the great hall. The warlord put his head back to watch the red mist rise and then gasped in amazement when the spirit didn't stop but simply passed straight through the ceiling as if it didn't exist. He leapt to his feet and, as fast as his limp would allow, he went to the spiral stairs and up the stone tower above and, when he didn't see the evil spirit there, he carried on to the wooden lookout tower that stood at the very top.

Panting for breath, the warlord burst out of the trapdoor and staggered onto the highest level in his castle. When he straightened up, he saw the red mist of the evil spirit pulsating near the edge of the wooden ramparts. She was looking up at the moon in the dark velvety sky.

The warlord stood still in the warm late evening air, breathing deeply to catch his breath and his cruel eyes narrowed as he waited to see what would happen next.

At first the evil spirit didn't move but the warlord became aware of sounds which could have been words coming from the hood of the evil spirit. If they were words, the sounds were not a language the warlord understood, but he did understand what they meant.

This was a spell being created, a spell he thought would bring immediate destruction to the village and the girl who had ruined his plans. He stood still as a rock listening and grinning a cruel smile all the time the evil spirit was chanting her strange, devilish utterances.

Finally, the evil spirit moved her sleeves to reveal two bony, withered arms with impossibly long fingers and curved nails on each thin finger. With these thin hands, the evil spirit pulled apart the front of her swirling mist, like she would have done had she been wearing a cloak, to reveal a red, pulsating ball. Using her long fingers and nails, she broke off a large portion of the viscous ball and then moulded it into an elongated spear-like shape, except it wasn't straight like a spear, it was zigzag in shape. It was, quite simply, a red lightning bolt, that pulsed with the evil spell that had created it, giving the impression it was somehow alive.

The warlord watched as the evil spirit fashioned the lightning bolt, and then held his breath as the evil one took the bolt in her long, thin bony hands and, drawing her left arm back hurled it impossibly high into the night sky, accompanying it with one last incomprehensible and ear-splitting shriek.

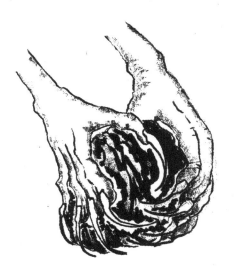

He watched as the bolt shot into the night sky, and then lost sight of it as it climbed higher and higher. After a minute of impatient waiting, he thought nothing was going to happen, and then there was a huge red explosion high up in the night sky.

Looking from below, it turned the moon into a

threatening red colour, and then the ear-splitting thunder crashed and, red lightning bolts lit up the sky, the wind began to rise and howl and finally sleet and snow began to fall. The spell was alive!

Life suddenly seemed much improved for the warlord.

HOLLY AND PINOFITA were sitting looking at the moon through their bedroom window when their world changed.

With the huge red explosion high in the sky and the thunder and lightning storm that followed as well as the high wind, both Holly and Pinofita stared in disbelief at the changing night sky, then at each other. Then, to their horror and amazement, the snow arrived in thick flakes but tinged red by the red light of the night sky above.

'What on earth has happened?' cried Holly to Pinofita. 'Why has everything changed to being like a terrible winter and why so quickly and why is the sky red?'

Holly looked with terrified eyes towards her little furry friend and felt her tummy churn with fright when Pinofita replied to her questions with just one whispered word. *'Evil!'*

26

THE KILLING STORM

THE WARLORD STARED at the evil spirit, who seemed to have shrunk somewhat in size after creating the red lightning bolt. With the snow falling all around him, he yelled at the red swirling figure, 'What have you done? You've brought a storm to the forest that will hurt me and my men just as much as it will the village and the girl!'

The spirit didn't reply. It just sank through the wooden floor of the tower, so the angry warlord had to follow down through the wooden tower and again down the stone spiral stairs until he arrived back in the great hall where he saw the red evil spirit floating in front of his chair, waiting for him.

The warlord limped to his chair then glared at the dark recess in the swirling red hood before him. 'What have you done?' he repeated.

After a few moments the cracked, hollow voice came out of the blackness of the face cavity in the hood. 'I have done what you wished for.'

'No, you haven't. You've brought misery to my home

just as much as you have to the girl and the village. And how is a storm going to rid me of that pest?'

Again, after a few moment's silence, the spirit replied, 'The storm spell is quite young. It still needs some more time to grow in strength and to find its real victim. The summer season has now been changed to a violent winter storm that is capable of killing the woodlands and crops. It will become so cold as to freeze a person, especially a small girl.'

'You've given us winter.' The warlord refused to be impressed.

The red mist shook its head. 'The real threat is that soon it will select its target. The huge storm will shrink in size but increase in intensity and it will move to remain over and around the person in your wish and anyone who stays near her. She is doomed to live, for the last few days left to her, in the grip of an ice storm and, as her family will stay with her, they will perish as well. She cannot live or even move properly in the killing storm. In fact, you would have to be an animal of the high forests to survive such conditions, and she is not!'

The warlord sat as still as a stone in his chair. He now saw the fiendish spell for what it was – a cruel spell that targeted the girl and, anyone who loved her enough to stay near her.

He smiled a cruel smile of pure evil satisfaction, relaxed in his chair and spoke to the evil spirit in a more respectful tone. 'Thank you, I now see the devilishness of your spell and approve. But you are not freed from your obligation to me until that annoying girl is finally gone. Do you understand?'

The evil swirling mass again seemed to nod the empty hood of the cape, then slowly floated higher towards the ceiling, resting there almost motionless as though trying to regain her strength after the exertion of creating and casting the killing storm spell.

27

UNDER ATTACK

HOLLY WAS STILL looking at Pinofita and struggling to come to terms with what she could see out of her bedroom window. She didn't understand what had happened or why, and she certainly didn't suspect that the growing red storm meant that she was under attack.

Then they heard her father's voice call urgently from below. 'Holly ... Holly if you are awake, please come down here now.'

Without any further ado, Holly put Pinofita on her shoulder and quickly climbed down the rickety ladder to join her parents, who stood close together in front of the dying fire embers. As Holly stood before them, her mother, with a grief-stricken voice said, 'Have you seen the sky outside and the horrific change in the weather?'

Holly nodded and said nothing.

Eryk remarked, 'The speed of the change is not natural. Winter should still be ages away after the crops are harvested and the berries and nuts of the forest gathered. Something is making this happen, but we have no idea what, do you?'

'Me?' said a surprised Holly, 'why on earth should I know?

'Well,' said Boda gently moving to hold her daughter's shoulders with both soft hands. 'You spend so much time in the forest and have a way with the animals and birds as well as having a very special little friend. We thought you might have an idea of what has caused this.'

'No, I'm sorry I don't,' said Holly, who was now near to tears.

Her mother hugged her closer, and Pinofita moved quickly to avoid being caught in the loving embrace. As they hugged one another, there came a knock on the front door of the small house. Quickly Eryk moved to open the door to be greeted by the very worried faces of two of his forester friends.

'Can you all come to the animal shelter, now please? We are all gathering to discuss what on earth has happened and what we should do,' said one of his friends.

'Of course. We'll be there as soon as we have our capes on,' replied her father closing the door against the unnatural cold blast of wind that entered the small cottage.

It was strange to go out wrapped up in their winter clothes. As Holly slung her cloak around her shoulders, she remembered the last time she'd worn it had been the very same day she'd made Pinofita, and her life had been changed forever. Taking a burning torch to light the way the three, well four of them, headed off through the snow for the village animal shelter. The animal shelter was where all the village livestock spent the winter months since it was protected from the worst of the weather and from hunting predators that came out of the forest and closer to the village in winter. It was also the biggest building in the village, so all the villagers had room to gather under the low thatch roof and to get out of the falling snow.

The meeting started with the usual clamour of voices calling for answers as to what had happened, and why a red storm would now appear in the northern sky? Of course, no one there could answer those questions, but someone did say that the red storm colour did seem brighter to the north than overhead. No one paid much attention to that comment so then the villagers began sorting out what they could do to protect themselves and their crops. Given the crops were not ready for harvesting, it was pointless thinking of trying to cut them and bring them in, unless it was just for animal feed. The berries and nuts in the forest again were not ready to be gathered, so no point doing that. In short, the villagers began to feel very scared at what lay ahead of them given the sudden and violent change in the weather.

It was at that point a new voice was added to the racket. The old man, who had been rescued by Edmund, the forest forager, and who had brought the terrifying message from the warlord, had been sleeping alone in the small house since Edmund was away in the forest. He had not been quick enough to join the start of the meeting since, after being roused, he had risen and dressed slowly, then made his way very slowly in the growing cold to the gathering in the animal shelter. Standing at the back of the crowd he now raised his voice and shouted, 'Maybe

I have a clue as to what has happened.'

Everyone stopped talking and turned to see who had spoken.

Gwillam moved forward until he was in the centre of the villagers. Then he stood upright and spoke slowly and clearly, but the words he uttered caused everyone gathered there to shudder.

He began, 'As you know I was taken to the warlord when I was first captured in the forest. It was there he gave me that horrible message about what he, his men and dogs were planning to do to this village.'

He paused to catch his breath and, as he did, most villagers nodded their heads in agreement, and everyone waited for the old man to continue.

'After he had given me the message to bring to you, he muttered something to himself which didn't make any sense at all when I first heard it.'

As he spoke, the wind outside continued to increase in force and the snow was falling a little harder, almost as though the storm was getter closer, but no one noticed.

The old man continued. 'I believe he said something like … *it was better to use me as a messenger of fear than use his wish.*'

'His wish?' several voices cried out. 'What on earth does that mean?'

In the hubbub of voices a strong, clear female voice rang out causing all other conversations and questions to stop. Boda stepped forward to stand next to the old man.

'I think we now have an idea, a possible answer as to why the season has changed so quickly and so dramatically. The warlord wanted us gone, and after we defeated him, he would want revenge and as soon as possible. This storm could drive us out of the village. It could be that he found a way to achieve what he and his hunters couldn't!'

'How would he do that? No man can control the weather.' A man at the back of the crowd sounded disbelieving.

Boda spoke to the whole crowd. 'I have to tell you that I think this is more than just bad weather. You all know me as someone who is not superstitious, but I stand before you tonight and say what we are experiencing has been created, not by human hand, but by something evil – and not of this world.'

The villagers were silent, apart from a few muffled sobs. Not a single voice spoke as people looked at one another with a growing fear on their faces. The foresters who had seen the aurochs hoofprints at the warlord's camp were nodding. Magic was not part of their lives, but they all knew the stories of the creatures in the forest. What worse things could someone like the warlord conjure?

Gwillam was the first to speak, 'The question now is what do we do? If it truly is magic, what can we do?'

Several voices called out that everyone should run. Others said no, what they should do is protect the animals by bringing them into the shelter in the morning, and then gather whatever food they could from the forest and store it.

Some of the foresters said they would bring more wood back to the village, so people had plenty of firewood to keep warm and others offered spare warm clothes to those who didn't have any. The mood of the village changed from one of defeat and became one of resistance and defiance to the dangers the storm had brought, and of gathering together to help one another survive for as long as they could. Feeling they had a good plan, the villagers agreed to close the meeting and to get together in the morning to start doing all the positive things they had talked about.

'Will we be all right?' asked Boda to her husband as they walked home through the snow with Holly and Pinofita.

'I don't know,' he sighed, 'the storm will ruin our crops, so what we will be able to gather in the forest tomorrow depends on how deep the snow is in the morning.'

'In that case we need a good night's sleep to be as strong as possible tomorrow,' said Boda as cheerily as she could manage but deep down she didn't feel very cheery, in fact, she was deeply worried.

28

A PLAN

IN HER SMALL bedroom Holly, still fully dressed, sat on her bed with Pinofita sitting on her cupped hand.

'I know it sounds unlikely, but when my mother says she thinks something that isn't human has created this storm, I think I believe her,' said Holly in hushed tones. She stared at Pinofita waiting for his answer.

After a few moments, the little mouse replied, 'I agree, it's magic – well, evil magic not the sort that created me – but something really bad that created this storm.'

Holly nodded slowly and added, 'Yes, but is this really meant to drive us out of the village? Or is there another reason for this storm?'

'Like what?' asked Pinofita.

'Well,' said Holly, 'we, or at least I, really caused the warlord to get very angry, and I did stab his foot with that sharp pole. Maybe all this is my fault.'

'No,' whispered Pinofita quickly. 'Of course it isn't. I think he wants revenge on the village, not just you. Remember his first message, it was all about getting rid of the villagers and the village so he could have these woods to himself.'

A worried silence grew between the two friends until it was broken by Holly, who leant forward and asked her friend a question. 'Would you help me to help the village please?'

Pinofita put his furry head to one side and looked at her questioningly.

Holly continued, 'Would you come with me into the forest to try and find where the warlord lives, and then a way to beat him and end this horrible storm?'

Pinofita looked at Holly with his big, shiny, black eyes and replied softly, 'Of course I will, you don't have to ask, because I hope you know I would do anything for you. I'd even gladly give my life to save yours.'

Holly looked at her small and very brave mousey friend, not fully realising the enormity of what he had just said. Instead, she found herself somehow thinking once again of the mysterious creature that had fought the dogs, and, even stranger, thinking of the dog-sized rock and the tree root which had tripped her as she'd been racing back to save him!

29

CHANGES IN THE FOREST

THE RED STORM was gathering in strength around the castle in the north. The unnatural wind howled through the woods with an intensity never felt before by the trees. The few animals and birds were completely taken by surprise with the severe change in the weather. They couldn't believe the wind and the snowstorm that now lashed the forest.

The birds were the first to react. They flew as far and as fast as they could away from the bitter teeth of the red storm. Then the smaller animals sought out their winter sleeping holes. To the north of the castle, the large red black deer huddled together and, in their family groups and small herds, moved further south to try to outrun the dropping temperature.

After the deer, there followed the killers of the high forest, the wolf pack. Sixteen grey wolves led by a huge leader who had been at the head of the pack for four years now. The huge grey leader knew of no natural enemy in these forests, other than the strange two-legged creatures who used to come to these woods to hunt his kin. But after the last encounter with them one dark night so many moons ago, even those strange creatures never came back again.

Further south in the forest, between the warlord's castle and the village where Holly lived, a lone figure was looking out from his wooden den of branches propped up against a tree trunk. It was Edmund, the young forest forager, who spent most of his time in the forest gathering honey, nuts, berries, roots and plants that were good to eat.

He had spent the night in one of his many dens scattered throughout this part of the woodland. He loved sleeping in the forest and waking up with the first rays of the summer sun in the eastern sky and the dawn chorus of the forest birds ringing in his ears.

When Edmund woke on this particular morning there was no bright yellow sun and no dawn chorus. Instead, there was a bitter wind howling through the trees and strange driving snow tinged a terrifying colour from the red sky above. He sat in his den confused and very worried. The question he had to answer was – do I sit here and wait or try to get to the village before the snow is too deep to travel?

To give himself some energy, and to make himself feel a bit better, he ate a portion of the honey and the roots he had already collected, sitting wrapped in his summer cloak, shivering and looking out onto a gathering snowstorm trying to think what to do for the best.

In fact, the decision was really made for him since the storm somehow intensified with the wind getting stronger, the temperature colder and the snow heavier.

Seeing what was happening in the small clearing in front of his shelter and the forest within his view, he sighed and moved back further into the den away from the wind and snow trying to make himself as comfortable and as warm as possible on his bed of bracken, with his cape firmly wrapped around him.

THE WARLORD WAS standing on the highest level of the wooden tower, dressed in a thick cloak to keep him warm in the driving snow and wind, staring at the red storm above and the swirling evil spirit who hovered to his right side.

'Well,' he demanded, 'has the storm rid me of the girl yet?'

Without turning to face the warlord the evil spirit spoke in her cracked and hollow voice. 'Not yet, but the storm is now intensifying and will soon become a killing storm. Also, it is trying to locate the girl, who is somewhere to the south of us in her village. If you look closely, the storm around us is now lessening as it moves away to where she is. In fact, the village where she lives should now be seeing the storm increase in strength and the snow fall become heavier.'

The warlord looked at the driving wind and snow and couldn't really decide if it was lessening or not. He didn't really care if it was or wasn't, all he wanted to know was that the girl who had lamed him was gone and hopefully her family and all the villagers with her.

With that cruel thought he turned and descended from the tower and went to inspect his remaining men, and how they were getting on with their preparations for another march south, and this time to destroy whatever remained of the village once the killing storm had done its terrible work.

THE NEXT MORNING, once her parents had left the cottage to go and help the other villagers, Holly quickly changed into her warm trousers, both her warm shirts, her green winter cape and high boots. Then she quickly checked the storage jars and put the two oatcakes and four acorns that she found in her pocket as supplies for their journey.

Before she left, she quickly fetched another wooden storage jar and sprinkled some of the contents on the table, then deftly moved her hand over the covering on the table top. Holly then rushed into the garden and looked for something she needed. Very quickly she found what she was looking for, but it was even better than she'd hoped. Back in the kitchen Holly placed what she had found in the garden on the table top. Her final job was to place some logs on the fire so her parents would come home to a warm cottage albeit an empty one.

With Pinofita safely in her hood the two small

adventurers set off towards the cold and snowy forest.

'Holly, Holly come down for some food and to hear the good news about the storm.'

When there was no answer, Holly's mother quickly went up the wooden ladder to peek into Holly's room. It was empty, but she noticed both her winter shirts were missing from their pegs on the wall and her winter trousers were not where they should have been either. She began to feel concerned, where on earth could Holly and Pinofita be? Once down in the main room she quickly checked by the door and, as she feared, Holly's green winter cape and high boots were also missing. Feeling a surge of real concern for the whereabouts of her daughter she walked back across the small room towards the table.

When Boda reached the table, something caught her eye causing her to stop and look down at the table surface. What she saw made her put both hands up to her mouth to try and suppress the cry of anguish that came from her lips. Her husband heard the muted cry and so dropped the logs he was carrying and ran to his wife's side.

'What is it?' he cried, 'what's the matter?'

Boda didn't speak. She was so upset she couldn't. All she did was to continue to stare at the tabletop. Eryk followed the direction of her gaze with his own eyes, and what he saw made him gasp with horror at the realisation of what it meant.

They both stood rooted to the spot and, staring at the tabletop with eyes transfixed on a scattering of white flour over the dark wood, but with a hastily drawn outline of a heart in it, and within the heart shape, a small sprig of holly with two bright berries on it, berries that shouldn't have been there since it was too early in the season for holly berries.

Boda turned to her husband and put both arms around him for comfort and support. 'They've gone into the storm haven't they, but what can they possibly do? She's only a girl with just a small mouse as a friend.'

Eryk hugged his wife even closer and, through his own silent anguish, he whispered, 'That's true, but he is a mouse who was made by the love Holly had for him, and by some strange but good magic, isn't he? We don't know where Pinofita really came from other than from the forest, and that's where they've gone now, to the forest, so maybe, just maybe there is a reason to hope.'

30

A COLD SNOWY
JOURNEY

'WHAT'S HAPPENED?' DEMANDED the warlord, 'has the killing storm spell worked? Am I rid of the girl?'

Without turning, the red spirit answered the warlord in her cracked and hollow voice. 'No, she is still alive, but something has happened as the storm is moving ever so slowly back to the north.'

'WHAT!' exclaimed the warlord, 'why would it do that? You said it would rest over the girl and rid me of her and maybe the family and the whole village as well?'

'I did, and it still does,' replied the red spirit.

Frustrated and angry, the warlord yelled, 'Explain yourself, can't you?'

At last, the red spirit turned to face the warlord and what she said in her hollow voice made the warlord feel the first cold trickle of fear slowly inch down his spine.

'The killing storm still rests over the girl as it can travel to follow once it has found its target, which it has. The reason the storm is heading north is that the girl is also heading north. She is not in her village, she is coming this way!'

HOLLY TRUDGED SLOWLY through the snow that was now almost up to Holly's knees making it very hard going. Once in the shelter of the trees, the snow wasn't so deep as the full summer canopy of the trees held much of the snow that was falling, so preventing it from reaching the forest floor. Walking now became easier and the gallant pair made better time as they began their journey north, but it was still a journey with no clear route or path to take them where they wanted to go since they didn't know where they were going!

After an hour of slow walking through the cold and the snow Holly said, 'Oh Pinofita, I'm not sure what to do or which way to go. Do you have any ideas?'

The little voice in her ear replied, 'I think we are heading the right way, but if we change direction a bit we will arrive at our special pine tree and I think that would be a good place to go to for a start.'

'Fine,' said Holly, 'to our pine tree it is.'

With now having a new purpose and specific place to go to, Holly felt a bit better and began to lose the helpless feeling that had been growing inside her during the first hour of their time in the wintery forest. So, with a renewed burst of energy, she changed direction a little and set her new course through the trees, trees that were strangely silent, as the birds had moved away from the bitter storm and the blanket of snow deadened all sound except the howling of the wind.

She couldn't understand it, maybe it was just a feeling, but with each step she felt strangely stronger. It was a comforting feeling. After almost another hour of trudging through the snow, at last they could see their goal standing in silent grandeur at the edge of the small clearing, as though challenging the storm to do its worst, which it was trying to do as the cold was now very intense turning Holly's lips and fingers blue.

IN THE GREAT hall of the castle, the warlord was pacing backwards and forwards in front of his fire yelling at the evil spirit that hung in the air just above him.

'How is it possible for this little girl to walk through the storm? You said it would be too cold and the snow too deep for that to happen. And why would she come north to me?'

The evil one was silent, as though thinking, but the warlord was so impatient, he yelled again, 'Speak to me, how can she move through the storm and why would she come here?'

The red spirit spoke with her hollow cracked voice, 'There is no explanation as to why she can walk through the snow drifts delivered by the killing storm, other than one.'

'So, what's that one reason?' shouted the warlord.

'The forest is helping her,' said the hollow voice, 'but it cannot save her since she cannot outrun the storm and, even though it will take longer, she is still doomed to perish in the cold and the snow.'

Slightly comforted by this reply the warlord stopped yelling and shouting and, after throwing himself down into his chair, he continued, 'So why is she coming this way?'

The swirling red mist of the evil one slowly turned to face the warlord and replied, 'I think she has realised what you have done, and is therefore trying to save her family and village from the storm by moving away from her home, so leading the storm back towards you: a valiant and brave gesture, but a futile one, as you will soon destroy the village once she, the storm and I are gone.'

The warlord accepted this explanation although the question did cross his mind as to how the girl would know this killing storm had come from him? He was also slightly worried now that the spell had not been as instantaneous as he had hoped and, for whatever reason, the object of his wish, that wretched girl, was still alive and now slowly coming north towards him.

The warlord would have been even more disturbed had the evil spirit told him her real concern. The concern was that, as the girl defied the killing spell storm, with every hour she continued to live, the strength of the evil spirit was weakened. The red storm had been created from a key element of the old witch, the red pulsating mass from within the swirling mist. This was the real force that gave the evil spirit her power and, the longer she was without it, the weaker she became, and the longer the girl defied the spell, the weaker the spell, the killing storm, also became.

AT THE BASE of the great pine tree Holly, with Pinofita still snuggled under her hood, stood and stared at the massive trunk. Now they were here, Holly was not sure what she should do; not sure what she should do in the next few minutes, or the next few hours, or the next few days. She began to think why on earth she, a girl and a little mouse, could defeat the warlord, and whatever had made the storm and the storm itself.

Without consciously deciding to do it, more because of some inner urge or feeling, slowly Holly approached the tree, as Pinofita had done when she had first brought him here. When she stood as close to the trunk as she could, without realizing what she was doing, she raised her arms as high as she could and placed both palms of her hands on the rough tree bark.

Closing her eyes, Holly asked herself the question what she should do next? Although no instant answer came to her, just feeling the tree bark under her hands was comforting, as it felt so strong and strangely warm despite the cold of the storm. She thought positively about what she had set out to do and, somehow, she began to sense a growing feeling inside herself – that she could do it. It was a wonderful feeling of hope.

Holly had no idea how long she had been standing touching the tree but, when she finally lowered her arms, she took several steps back and turned her head to ask Pinofita, 'Are you all right, ready to go on?'

Pinofita didn't turn his head towards Holly. He just stared at the tree trunk and, in an excited whisper, said to Holly.

'Don't be afraid but look at the trunk of the tree!'

31

A FOREST FRIEND

FURTHER TO THE north, Edmund was still marooned in his den, although the thick cap of snow had helped him by insulating the den from the biting wind. He had watched the storm all day from the relative safety of his shelter, and at times, he imagined the deep red centre to be moving south getting ever closer to the village.

However, when he looked up at the red sky now, he thought that the centre of the storm was moving slightly back towards him once more. He looked at the sky and felt glum and very alone, even though he usually enjoyed being on his own.

He took stock of the supply of food he had stored in his foraging bags and thought, if he was careful, he could make the food last at least another three days, although he really didn't want to be trapped for that amount of time. For drinking water, he had already finished the water he had brought with him in his animal skin bottle, but all he had to do was to carefully push some clean snow into the bottle, hug it to his warm body and, in a few minutes, the snow melted, and he had more water.

His biggest problem was boredom, he was at a loss of what to do to keep himself amused, so he told himself all the stories he could remember about the legends and myths of the forest. The scary ones he told himself during the daylight hours; and, just before he went to sleep, he recounted the nice, gentle ones about tree elves and nice things like that.

ERYK WENT TO help bring some more wood to the village, but Boda stayed in their cottage sitting at the table clutching the sprig of holly and staring at the heart shape on the table. She wanted her daughter safe at home, but she was also experiencing a growing feeling of admiration for what Holly was trying to do. She thought of how Holly had succeeded when the warlord was about to attack the village, and nobody expected her to achieve what she had done that night, so maybe there was a chance this would be the same. She also remembered her husband's words about Pinofita and of him being created by good magic and of coming from bits of the forest himself, the same place where he and Holly were now.

'Yes,' she said aloud, 'they can do it, they can.'

And, with that new resolve, she felt stronger and able to face whatever the next few hours or days brought.

WHEN PINOFITA HAD said, 'Don't be afraid but look at the trunk of the tree,' Holly had held her breath and, summoning all her courage, turned her head and looked straight ahead at the massive tree.

At first, all Holly could see was the wide, rough barked trunk of the massive pine tree where a few moments ago she had stood with her hands raised up pressed against it. The harder she looked, the more it was just a tree, even when her little friend said, 'Do you see it, can you see it now?'

All she could see was the solid, rough textured tree trunk. In frustration Holly lifted her gaze slightly higher and then froze, not believing what she was seeing.

She couldn't speak, in fact she could barely breathe, so impossible was what she was sure she could now see. Within the bark of the tree trunk, two large green eyes looked down kindly on the little pair of adventurers.

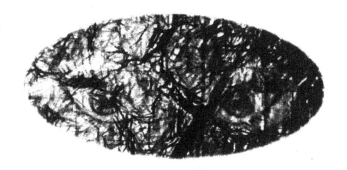

Holly didn't move a muscle, she just watched and waited. After a few moments, when Holly had become a little bit more believing of what she was seeing, the area of tree bark around the eyes began to change. From a rough textured bark, it seemed to dissolve and, in its place, a face around the eyes began to form. A face that smiled down on Holly, reassuring her that whoever, or whatever, this figure was, it was a friend, a friend to be trusted.

After the face was fully formed, the whole smiling head, complete with long golden green shimmering hair, with an array of flowers intertwined in it, then appeared. Holly stared in complete astonishment at the image taking shape before her very eyes. She wanted to run, and she wanted to stay but the kindly smile made her believe she should stay, which she did, reassured as well by the warm little body nestling in her neck.

The image before Holly didn't stop evolving; it kept on growing until a tall female form draped in a long flowing, shimmering green cloak of leaves and flowers finally emerged from the tree, and stood tall before Holly, looking down on her and smiling. Holly smiled a nervous little smile back and waited. Whilst all this was happening, Holly was oblivious to the wind, snow and the cold of the red storm. It was as if she had been lifted out of the wintery forest and become protected from the stormy elements in a soft bubble of warmth and love.

When the beautiful flower-adorned figure spoke, Holly couldn't see the lips moving, but she could hear words in her head as clearly as if the wondrous figure had spoken to her normally.

'Hello Holly,' said the kindly voice in her head, 'at last we meet face to face.'

Holly, of course, had no idea this same face had been watching her for many years from the trees, bushes and flowers of the forest as well as from the sky.

Holly was oblivious to the fact that all her kind deeds in the forest had been observed, and they had eventually marked her out as someone special, a friend of the woodlands and forest, and all the creatures living there.

Holly tried to speak aloud but the words she spoke seemed just to form in her mind not her mouth.

'Hello,' said Holly in her mind, but the widening smile in front of her let Holly know her words had been heard.

'I hope you have been enjoying the company of your new friend Pinofita?' the voice in Holly's head continued.

'I have, very much thank you,' replied Holly.

Then a key question she had always wanted to know the answer to struck her, and she thought, 'Was it you who gave me the shimmering powder on my birthday to make him come alive and talk?'

The beautiful head before her nodded gently, causing the long hair to move and the flowers in it to bob with it.

'Oh, thank you so much for that,' thought Holly, 'he is the best present and friend ever!'

'I'm delighted you like him, and that he is such a good friend,' replied the gentle voice in Holly's head, and then continued, 'now, why are you both in the forest in the middle of this terrible storm?'

Holly heard the words and replied with the thought, 'We are trying to find the castle of the warlord somewhere in the north, and then we need to defeat the thing that has created this storm and so end this horrible weather.'

The face before Holly seemed to shimmer and fade a bit then the voice in her head continued. 'You have set yourselves a lot of difficult things to do, so I would like to help you both if you will allow me?'

Holly just nodded repeatedly and, in her mind replied, 'Oh yes please, yes please, for anything you can do to help us.'

The flower-adorned face smiled and reaching out from within her flower and leaf cape, placed something into Holly's hand.

'Take this, use it sparingly when you need to and remember me to an old friend.'

Holly didn't really understand what she was being told, she knew all the words that now reverberated around her head but, when used together like they just had, it left her struggling to follow what she was being asked to do. She was so confused she didn't even ask a question with her mind. She just continued to stand there and listen.

The lovely figure before her continued to talk in Holly's mind. 'Trust which path you need to take and, whilst I will help where I can, I believe it will be you Holly, and your furry friend, who will make the most difference in saving the forest.'

Again, Holly was so awe stricken by the words she heard that she continued just to stand very still and stare unbelievingly into the green eyes before her.

'Go now and be brave but above all else remember, never lose hope, for without hope, all becomes darkness and despair.'

With those last words of encouragement, long slim fingers gently brushed against Holly's hand, leaving Holly with a strange tingly feeling all through her body. The voice within Holly's head vanished and, as Holly began to feel the cold wind again, a strong blast of icy air blew and the figure before Holly was blown away in a swirl of snow, flowers and leaves.

She and Pinofita stood once again in the freezing snow before the huge pine tree, with the storm seeming to intensify directly overhead.

'DID THAT REALLY happen?' Holly asked her furry friend who was still nuzzled up against her neck. Pinofita moved a bit to one side and looked at Holly and his little head with two big ears slowly nodded. Still not quite sure it had happened Holly then became conscious of something cold and hard in the palm of her hand. Looking down Holly saw a tube of crystal containing some glowing, shimmering golden powder, securely fastened with a stopper of golden green hair. It looked like the same powder that had brought Pinofita to life on her birthday.

Shaking her head in disbelief, Holly carefully put the tube in her warm pocket and then looked back towards the pine tree.

'Thank you,' she said aloud, her spoken words being whipped away by the cold, cold wind.

In the fading light, she and Pinofita turned and headed north almost as though Holly knew instinctively exactly which path through the trees would lead them to where they needed to go.

32

THE FOREST INTERVENES

THE WARLORD WAS out on the roof of the wooden lookout tower again. He was with the evil red spirit, both looking towards the deep red centre of the storm to the south that was behaving in a very strange way. The centre of the storm seemed to be unsure of where it should be over the forest; it wavered again and again.

'Why is it doing that?' demanded the warlord.

The evil one hesitated and then said, 'It has lost the child; I can feel the hesitancy it has on where exactly it has to be.'

The warlord was beside himself with anger and disbelief.

'What do you mean, it's lost the child?' he roared at the red spirit.

'I mean exactly that, the spell targeting the child is currently blindfolded in some way, and has lost her,' said the hollow voice.

'What on earth can blindfold a storm?' the warlord screamed. 'Tell me.'

The evil spirit turned to the warlord and replied, 'I can put it a clearer way. The child is currently protected from the effects of the storm by some strange but very powerful force. That's why the storm has lost sight of her, for now.'

The warlord tried to understand what the evil one had just said. It didn't make sense. He was the one with the evil spirit of the witch, who had cast the killing spell in the form of a storm and the village, especially the foolish girl, had no such evil ally. So what was protecting the child from the storm?

Instead of raising his voice again, he took two steps towards the floating evil spirit and asked in a more normal but still threatening voice, 'What do you think has happened, and what do we do now?'

The red spirit waited for a few drawn-out seconds. Then the cracked voice replied, 'The forest has intervened, but only for a few minutes. I can feel the storm is now steadying over the girl again, and the killing cold will return to stop her.'

The warlord looked darkly at the evil one and smiled grimly. Then he turned and descended to the great hall. Once there, he didn't go to his chair by the fire. He went to where his remaining men were eating their evening meal. He entered the room and, before any of the men could stand in recognition of their master, he spoke to them quietly and coldly.

'Have your weapons sharpened and ready, for tomorrow we need to act.'

He then turned and left the room, leaving the eight hooded men looking at one another with anxious stares. If they had to act, that meant the evil spirit had not removed the villagers and the girl and, if that unearthly thing couldn't do it, how on earth could they?

33

THE FREEZING RIVER

ALL THE VILLAGERS had gathered yet again, since more of them now agreed that the storm seemed to be lessening in ferocity. Just getting together to talk about the changes in the storm also helped their morale, as did the different reports of what people had done to prepare to sit out the storm. Only two of the villagers didn't look so happy as they stood with the crowd. Holly's mother and father who tried to sound positive and to look relieved at the lessening of the storm's force but, in their hearts, they were distraught.

As they stood there holding hands alongside their friends and neighbours, the old man spoke again, his voice easier to hear now that the wind had subsided quite a bit.

'I think we can see the storm has died down from what it was, which is really good for us all. I have no idea why this happened and why it happened so quickly, but the deep red centre of the storm has moved further away, back towards the north from where it came.'

He then said something that made Holly's parents

grip each other's hand more tightly.

'To me, it is almost like the storm has been drawn away from the village and lured back into the forest by something. Let's hope it continues to move further away in the night. By morning light we will know.'

Boda and Eryk walked slowly back home with heavy hearts as they went over the words Gwillam had spoken over and over again. They had tried to follow Holly's tracks from the village, but the deep snow had made that impossible. The whole village was trapped here.

'Can he be right; is the storm being drawn away?' asked Boda.

'I have no idea,' replied Eryk, 'I think he is right in that the storm is moving away to the north, but if that means it is following Holly, then I don't want him to be right.'

HOLLY AND PINOFITA had made good progress on their journey north since leaving the pine tree. However, the cold was getting colder, and Holly was beginning to feel she couldn't go on. Every step in the deepening snow was harder than the last and she knew she needed to rest soon as she felt her strength and energy disappearing fast.

Pinofita sensed his friend was weakening and so quietly spoke into her ear. 'Holly, let's find some shelter for the night and then we can carry on tomorrow.'

'Good idea' replied a weary Holly, 'but where do we shelter for tonight to get out of this biting wind and driving snow?'

Pinofita looked ahead from the shelter of Holly's hood and said, 'In a hollow tree, or in thick bushes anywhere that gives us a bit of shelter.'

In truth, he couldn't see either of those places, all he could see was huge snowflakes driving towards them on the teeth of a freezing wind. The more he thought about their situation, and what or who might have caused it, made him angry. They should not be attacking his friend Holly like this.

Sometime later Holly, who had continued to trudge through the snow and freezing wind, slipped and tumbled forward into a deep snow drift that had formed in the space between the mounds of earth dug out of the ground by a family of badgers some time ago.

Holly gasped aloud as she landed, more out of surprise than being hurt. The snow was deep and soft, and Holly's only thought was of struggling up and continuing her journey, but her furry friend's voice stopped her.

'Holly, this could be the shelter we need tonight. Can you make it a bit deeper so we can get out of the wind a little bit more?'

Holly looked at the snow around them and began digging with her hands and pushing the snow to the top edge of the hollow to make it more protected from the storm. After ten gruelling minutes of digging and moving snow around them, Holly had created a hole they could crouch in and get out of the worst of the storm.

Exhausted, Holly sat in the snow hole and tried to get

her breath back. Pinofita had encouraged her all the time she had been digging and he now tried to cheer her up.

'Thank you, Holly, we have made a lot of progress all day since we saw the lady in green at the pine tree, and this snow shelter will really help to keep us safe and warm tonight.'

'Do you really think so?' asked Holly, sounding worn out and dejected.

'Of course,' Pinofita replied, 'it will make all the difference, you'll see. Now, do you have any supplies in your cape pocket?'

Holly's eyes brightened. 'Yes!'

Holly retrieved the oatcakes and acorns and having passed two acorns to Pinofita, she took one of her oatcakes in her cold fingers and they both sat huddled in their new snowy home and slowly ate their meagre supper whilst the storm raged overhead, and the temperature dropped even further.

THE EVIL SPIRIT floated in front of the warlord, who was again back in his chair in front of the blazing fire in his great hall.

'Speak, what news of the girl?' he demanded.

The evil one spoke in her cracked and hollow voice that echoed eerily around the stone walls.

'The storm has stopped the progress of the child, she is deep in the snow and, as the killing storm continues through the night, it will complete the spell and your wish will be delivered.'

The warlord's eyes narrowed, and a cruel smile broke out on his dark veined face, then his mouth opened and he laughed an evil short laugh of victory.

'Ha haaaa, at last revenge for what she did to me and my men. When will we know for sure the spell and the wish are complete?'

The spirit continued to hover in the firelight that made it look redder than it really was since, in truth, the spirit had become paler and slightly weaker with every step Holly had made northwards that day.

'Tomorrow morning, when there is no further movement of the storm, and the child remains deep in the snow, then we will know. Then your wish is completed and I will be set free.'

The warlord looked sideways at the evil spirit and in a slow and threatening voice said. 'You will only be set free once I am sure my wish has been granted, then and only then.'

The red mist again seemed to nod the empty hood towards the warlord as a sign of agreement and then floated upwards towards the ceiling rafters where it remained motionless, almost like it was sleeping.

DEEP IN THEIR snowdrift hollow, Holly and Pinofita had finished their supper but having brought no drink with them, they had to wash it down with mouthfuls of snow, which when melted in their mouths allowed the very cold water to run down their throats. Sort of refreshing but very, very cold!

The weary pair settled down as best they could in the snow, Pinofita being the luckiest as he had Holly's warm hood to snuggle into. For Holly it was different, where the snow had melted around her, the water had soaked into her clothes and she was feeling wet and cold, very cold, in fact she was dangerously cold. The temperature under the howling storm dropped even lower, and this, combined with the snow and her wet clothes, had a dramatic effect on her. She was getting too cold to survive. It was indeed a killing storm!

Snuggled in her hood Pinofita was very aware of the sudden change in Holly's condition. He thought of the cruel forces of the storm, and how they were trying to hurt his beloved friend. The more he thought about it, the angrier he became, something, or someone, was trying to harm his friend Holly and there was only him, a small mouse, to protect her.

He felt the hair on his body rise and his eyes began to burn with the anger he felt towards whatever was hurting Holly. The only thing he could see and hear trying to harm his friend was the storm with its freezing wind and snow, so that's what he focused his anger towards. He stepped out from the shelter of Holly's hood and, standing on the snow next to her hood, he glared up at the storm, his hair on end and his eyes burning red in anger and defiance.

In her delirious dream, Holly imagined herself being

swept along by a freezing strong current of water. Her hands were met by a numbing cold wherever she put them. Her feet she could not feel, and her face was so cold she thought it might shatter if she touched it, like ice on a puddle when you step on it. It was a never-ending rush of swirling turbulence of wet, freezing cold waves that washed over her wherever she moved her body.

As her temperature dropped even lower, another strange element in her dream-like trance happened, and it was not a good one. Slowly, images of her life, her memories, came to the front of her mind and then seemed to dissolve and disappear like smoke blown away by a breeze only to be replaced by another happy image that also dissolved and vanished. The truth was Holly was now so cold her body was gradually shutting down and with every evaporating memory, her life was slowly ebbing away. There was nothing she could do to stop it, all she could do was suffer terribly, as she inched closer to the seemingly inevitable freezing blackness that threatened to envelop and crush her.

Then, in her dream, one of her hands suddenly felt a tuft of what she thought was grass, grass that maybe grew at the side of this fast flowing freezing water. Her body reacted and, in desperation, her fingers managed to feebly grip the grass and, in her freezing trance she was amazed to realise that the grass she held onto was not freezing, it was warm!

Deep within her freezing dream-like state, a tiny light flared in the encroaching, crushing blackness, the first tiny light of hope.

In her dream Holly slowly became aware of being

surrounded by, and seemingly entangled within, this warm life-saving grass. Her dream changed from one of cold desperation to survive, to a feeling of relief as she snuggled ever deeper into the warm embrace of the grasses surrounding her. Her breathing became deeper and more regular. Her face lost its deathly pale colour and her hands and lips lost their numbing blue colour. She finally relaxed and lost herself in the unexpected, but very welcome, warmth and softness that enveloped her.

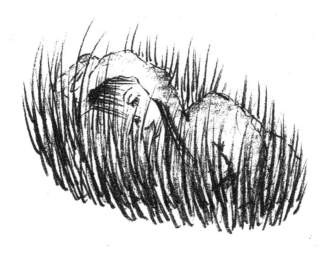

As she felt her body slowly gain warmth, her mind stopped fighting the cold that had surrounded her and went back to a previous dream of a strange mound covered in wild flowers and bathed in sunlight, with birds singing overhead. But now it had the lovely face from the pine tree smiling out at her from within the flowers. It was a lovely dream.

Back in the snow-filled hollow, Pinofita wrapped his huge body and tail around his friend and hugged her to him to protect and warm her, whilst his red-hot ruby eyes blazed defiance at the storm above that had tried to take Holly from him. He stayed like that for as long as his anger burned. Whilst Holly slept peacefully, as she did through the rest of the night, she was unaware of who had saved her.

34

THE CHILD
STILL LIVES

AS DAWN BROKE the next day, Boda was already up, dressed and looking out of her bedroom window, still clutching the small sprig of holly she had found on the table.

It was as the old man had thought, the storm intensity around the village had decreased and the deep red of the centre of the storm was much further north, taking the snow and the numbing cold with it. As she looked at the sky, she felt the storm had grown smaller but somehow intensified in colour. So engrossed had she become looking at the red storm she didn't notice Eryk had woken and risen, until he stood next to her and put his arm around her.

'Have you been looking out of the window all night?' he asked gently.

'No, from just before the dawn broke but look, the storm is different.'

'It most certainly is,' replied Eryk with an edge of relief and excitement in his voice, 'maybe we won't have to consider leaving the village and hopefully we won't need all the preparations we struggled to do yesterday. There is hope for the village after all.'

'If Gwillam was right, does that mean Holly is out there under the centre of that?' asked Boda with a nervousness in her voice.

Eryk squeezed her tighter and said reassuringly, 'We don't know if, like all storms, this moves as the wind pushes it. She and Pinofita could be in a different part of the forest and may have been sheltering in one of the many places I know she knows to avoid the wind and snow. We'll just have to wait and see what today brings.'

'Waiting,' sighed Boda, 'it's the waiting and the not knowing that are the hardest things to bear.'

SLOWLY HOLLY WOKE from what had started out as a terrible freezing cold nightmare, which turned into one of the nicest dreams she had ever had. She felt rested and strong – and ready to carry on with their quest. All thoughts of stopping and going home were now banished from her mind. She whispered 'Good morning Pinofita, how are you, did you sleep well?'

A sleepy voice answered immediately, 'I'm fine, just a little tired as I didn't get much sleep last night. It must have been the storm keeping me awake.'

'Never mind,' replied a happy Holly, 'you can sleep in my hood as we go further north.'

'Thank you, that would be lovely. But please wake me if there is any trouble or danger.'

'Of course,' replied Holly, 'now hold tight as I stand up and climb out of here.'

Just after dawn Holly, with Pinofita snuggled in her hood, climbed out of the snow hollow. Holly couldn't quite understand why the hole was so much bigger and wider than it had been when she had made it the night before. She didn't spend too much time worrying about that small but interesting fact. She just gritted her teeth and set out in the sure knowledge she was going in the right direction.

In her hood, Pinofita settled down to a well-earned rest. He had glared at the storm all night, his eyes burning a brighter red than the sky overhead. It had taken a lot of his strength to manage a night like he had just had, so sleep was what he needed, and sleep he did.

THE RED SPIRIT was still motionless near the ceiling of the great hall when it jolted, as though shot by an arrow. If it could have gasped it would have done, for what had happened was that the storm, which had been stationary all night now suddenly moved, and the red evil spirit had felt it. Immediately, the evil one rose up through the ceiling, through the wooden tower and up onto the highest level of the castle from where it could view the forest. The storm was moving, slowly – at the speed of a child walking through deep snow. But it should not have been moving. The red spirit knew the killing storm had been at its height all through last night and should have completed the warlord's one wish.

But it was moving. The child still lived!

The issue now was that the evil spirit would have to inform the warlord. She knew he was not going to be happy.

35

LOST IN THE SNOW

HOLLY WAS MOVING as quickly as she could, but despite the tree canopy preventing a lot of the snow from reaching the forest floor, the snow was a real hindrance and progress was slow. Also, the storm didn't seem to be getting any weaker. After three hours of slowly trudging, Holly became aware for the first time since entering the forest gripped by the storm, of another voice other than her own or Pinofita's.

It wasn't a threatening human voice – for she had feared the warlord might be in the forest looking for her – it was a frightened whine, a whine that said the owner of the voice was lost and scared and probably too young to be on their own in the forest in the storm.

Holly whispered, 'Pinofita, are you awake?'

No answer came from her hood so Holly slowly stepped forward looking through the falling snow as to where the plaintive whine might be coming from. 'It must be close,' thought Holly but where on earth could it be? She was faced by snowy thickets on the left, her as yet untrodden path to the north straight ahead through the trees, and to the right a large fallen tree now covered by a layer of snow.

'Under the branches of the fallen tree,' whispered a familiar voice in her ear.

'Oh, you are awake,' smiled Holly now looking very carefully at the tangle of snow-covered branches. There it was again, she heard the whine, this time smaller and more hesitant than before.

'Oh no,' said Holly, 'whatever it is, is afraid of us!'

'Think kind words,' said Pinofita, 'don't use your human voice, think of the things you would say to comfort whatever it is, and move even slower than you are towards the branches and direct the words in your mind to that dark space under the branches.'

Holly thought 'Don't be afraid little one we are here to help you, not hurt you. We are lost in the storm as you are, so maybe we can help each other. Don't be afraid and, if you can, let me see where you are.'

Holly waited a few moments. Then to her amazement and delight a small furry grey head with two pointed ears, two bright amber eyes and a wet black nose peered out from under the branches where Pinofita had suggested the lost creature was hiding.

She didn't know what the creature was, but she did know it was lost, scared and probably hungry. Holly also thought it was a wonder such a small creature had survived out in the storm alone, away from its mother. What Holly didn't know, was that the little grey creature in front of her was from the high forests, where this sort of weather was not uncommon. It was a grey wolf cub!

Cautiously, the little creature stepped out from under

the bushes and padded slowly towards the outstretched hand. Holly held her breath as the cub's muzzle came ever closer. Time almost stopped for her, as through the falling, freezing snow, the wet black nose touched her hand causing that strange tingling feeling to course through her entire body. It was the same feeling as when she had met the lady with the lovely smile and the flowing gold, green hair from the pine tree.

Once the touch of fingers and nose had happened, the wolf cub seemed to understand that Holly was a friend and would do him no harm. So, like he would if he greeted his own kind, he stepped forward and, with head facing down, he moved to rub forehead and cheeks with Holly. Instinctively Holly did the same and, as their foreheads and faces rubbed together, a warmth swept over her like a warm ray of sunshine on a hot summer's day.

THE WARLORD WAS beside himself with anger and blind rage, he couldn't believe what the evil spirit had just said to him. With his dark-veined face contorted in a snarl, he threw the drinking vessel he had been using at the red spirit floating in front of him. The mug hurtled towards the evil spirit, who didn't move. There was no need to since the heavy vessel passed right through the swirling mist of the shape where the body should have been, to then clatter against the stone wall behind it. The red swirling mist just reformed itself as if nothing had happened. This infuriated the warlord even more.

He was panting with the effort of having been shouting abuse at the evil spirit for the past few minutes. All his respect had gone for this swirling essence of the evil witch, and now he knew he couldn't trust that she could deliver his one wish. He would have to take matters into his own hands. With that he turned on his heel and walked towards where his men were busy sharpening their weapons.

In his fury, the warlord had also missed the fact that the evil spirit had shrunk a tiny bit more and was just a little paler than the previous night. The evil one could feel the weakening in her powers and knew that, with every hour that passed and every mile the child drew nearer the castle, her evil essence would suffer the slow fate of invisibility and, finally a crushing black oblivion. She needed to do something to prevent that from happening to her. The child had to be stopped.

IF IT WAS all anger and rage at the castle, at that very moment it was just the opposite in the village. People could now see that the red storm was moving north and back to where it had come from. The snow had stopped falling and the icicles that had formed on every roof edge were dripping water as they melted quickly in the weak yellow sun that was now beginning to shine through. Where there had been only sorrow and despair, there was now laughter and hope. Even Holly's parents joined in the happy laughter and chatter, feeling a quiet pride and wonder that perhaps Holly was involved in this escape. Then Boda would feel a small prickle from the sprig of holly she had put in her skirt pocket, and it brought a frown to her face and a veil of sadness fell over her eyes.

Eryk put his hand gently over hers. 'What we need now,' he said quietly, 'is exactly what we needed when Holly and Pinofita had left the village to go to the warlord's camp to discover his attack plan.'

'What's that?' asked his wife.

He looked her in the eyes and, squeezing her hand, said, with hopeful determination, 'a sign, any sign.'

If they could have seen Holly at that very moment, they would have been totally surprised but would have laughed out loud. The snow was still falling around the little girl with the mouse in her hood, and now a wolf cub, whose keen nose had smelt the remaining oatcake in Holly's pocket, was pushing his hungry face into her cape trying to find the source of the food.

Holly squealed with laughter at the sudden push of the wolf cub's nose as she realised what he was up to.

All right little one, she thought, *we can share this one last piece of food.*

The cub seemed to understand so stopped pushing

and sat back on his haunches and waited, with drool dripping down from his mouth. Holly quickly retrieved the oatcake, which was a bit bashed by now, but still looked very appetizing to the cub. She broke the oatcake into three pieces and then put one of the pieces on the snow in front of the cub.

He quickly leant forward and devoured it in one gulp. Holly ate another of the pieces and then held out the third and last piece on the palm of her hand and offered it to the cub. The cub stood, took one pace forward, then softly took the proffered morsel in his mouth. To Holly's delight, he gently licked the crumbs from her hand.

Holly asked Pinofita if he wanted an acorn, but the little mouse said he would wait for supper until he ate it. As they sat in the snow, Holly, with her word thoughts, introduced the cub to Pinofita. At first the cub looked very interested in Pinofita since he was still hungry and, unseen by Holly, the burning red eyes of Pinofita told the cub to behave. This warning combined with Holly's kind-thought words ensured the wolf cub understood and didn't do something Holly, and especially Pinofita, would find upsetting.

With Pinofita in her hood and her eyes looking keenly ahead along the path north, she set off once again through the trees, wind and snow with the wolf cub slowly walking at her side.

THE WARLORD CALLED for his men to be ready to receive instructions to defend the castle and themselves against a force that was coming north through the storm and snow to attack them. Before the warlord addressed his armed men, he went once again onto the top level of the wooden tower with the evil spirit. When he stood on the top of the tower the warlord demanded that the spirit show him precisely the direction the girl would approach from. Raising a swirling sleeve, the evil spirit drew a bony arm out of the depths of the mist and, with one long talon-like nail, pointed in the direction she felt the pure spirit of the girl was coming from.

The warlord noted the direction, and from it, he could recollect key features in that part of the forest where it would be best to set an ambush. There was one clearing with a dense thicket on one side and large rocks to the other side that would provide cover for his men.

Armed with this information, the warlord returned to where his hunters had gathered and began to address them.

'Men,' he shouted, 'the time has come to prepare ourselves for an attack from the village in the south. We believe the attacking force to be able to resist the power of the storm and expect it to arrive in the next few days. We shall act now to lay an ambush they will not suspect. Four of you will go to the rock-strewn clearing half a day's march from here and lay an ambush to capture the person who is coming to attack us. Remember you do not kill; you capture and return here with the person alive.'

The hunters looked at each other in surprise. They

had been expecting the warlord to say that they had to prepare to do battle with the large group of villagers who had routed them in their camp some days ago. To hear it was a person, just one person, coming to attack them filled them with bemused confidence. Of course they could easily capture whoever it was. Suddenly it wasn't so bad. All their fears of the past few hours evaporated. They began to smile and grin about what lay before them.

The warlord then detailed the remaining men to stand watch on the wooden ramparts by the castle gates and patrol the inner area of the castle. Some of the armed men thought this excessive for the ambush, capture and return to the castle, alive, of just one person. However, nobody asked why such precautions were necessary, since the warlord was never challenged by his men, they were too scared of him.

The hunters detailed to lay the ambush ran to gather their weapons, supplies and equipment. Then, in a ragged sort of formation, they marched out of the castle and across the blackened clearing, which was now white with lying snow, and entered the forest. It was a short fast march to the clearing identified as the best place to set the ambush and they were keen to get everything set up before nightfall and then sit in hiding, waiting for this one person who was coming to attack them. Whoever it was must be mad they thought, mad but very, very brave!

36

KILLERS OF THE HIGH FOREST

BY EARLY EVENING Holly and the wolf cub were exhausted. They had walked as far as they could in the driving snow and the storm still seemed to be overhead and almost as ferocious as ever. They had not eaten again as Holly didn't have any more food and all they had to drink was ice cold water from snow they melted in their mouths. Holly called a halt to their march when she saw a large old tree with a huge cave-like hollow at its base.

'Over there,' she thought, 'we can rest in some dry shelter for a while.' The other two travellers seemed to understand her thoughts and so, in a few moments, Holly was safely in the hollow as far from the entrance as she could get with Pinofita still nestling against her neck and the wolf cub huddled up against her for company. So tired were the three of them, they almost instantly fell asleep huddled together.

What they didn't know was that a few miles back along the path they had travelled through the forest, fifteen grey creatures were carefully following their fading tracks and faint scent trail. With noses to the snowy ground and trotting swiftly on silent pads, the wolf pack was quickly closing in on the two-legged creature they believed had taken their cub. They made no sound as they moved ghost-like through the trees, but their amber eyes burned bright and revenge pulsed in their veins.

Holly, Pinofita and the wolf cub were all woken at the very same moment, the moment the huge grey leader of the wolf pack raised his head to the raging storm and howled into the night only a few yards from the hollow tree. A sound that froze the blood of any prey animal close enough to hear it. It had the same effect on Holly who woke with a start then stared open-mouthed out of the opening of the hollow tree, initially unable to move a muscle. Pinofita felt the hairs on his body rise and his eyes begin to burn but the wolf cub howled his somewhat timid response and trotted happily out of the tree hollow and into the semicircle of amber eyes that faced him.

Something made Holly's entire body tingle, as the sound of the leader's howl echoed through the storm, and finally died away into the night. She reached up and, taking Pinofita out of her hood, she put him on the ground and asked him to please stay where she had put him. In her normal voice, with no trace of a tremor or stammer she said 'Please stay here and wait for me. This is something I feel I have to do, alone.'

Pinofita looked at Holly and replied, 'You do what you have to, and I'll do what I have to, but I will only do as you ask until …'

'Until what?' asked Holly, but Pinofita didn't answer. He just looked at his brave friend and hoped.

The wolf howl rent the night again but, somehow the tone had changed. It was now challenging and more threatening. As the sound of the howl slowly died in the snowstorm, Holly emerged from the tree hollow and stood in the moonlight with the freezing snow swirling around her. She could see the semicircle of amber eyes and, close to her on her left, she could see the wolf cub standing next to an adult wolf she thought might be his mother. However, what really commanded Holly's attention was the huge grey wolf directly in front of her, his two amber eyes burning with hate for the two-legged creature. She heard a low threatening growl rumbling deep in his throat.

Holly began trying to talk to the wolf leader in her mind.

My name is Holly, she thought, *I did not hurt the cub, I helped him a bit. I befriended him when he was lonely, and he shared some food with me, then followed me as I walked through the forest in the storm that is still raging above and around us.*

As far as Holly was concerned, the huge grey wolf was still just staring at her but not moving any closer, which she thought was a good thing. In fact, the low threatening growls from the grey leader had stopped, and now he stood motionless and silent, his amber eyes fixed on a point in front of him.

If you had been unlucky enough to have been standing in front of that hollow tree next to the grey pack leader and looking straight ahead at the green-caped girl

205

standing bravely facing the wolf pack in the swirling, freezing snow, you would have also seen something else that would have commanded your attention, as it did now to the alpha wolf.

Just to the left of where Holly stood in the falling snow but, from within the dark depths of the hollow at the base of the tree from which she had recently emerged, you would have seen two huge ruby red eyes burning through the darkness. Two eyes that bored into the amber eyes of the wolf in front of Holly, eyes that conveyed more messages than words could have done in the short space of time the wolf had been staring at them. The amber eyes of the wolf looked into the blazing red eyes and understood.

The effect on the wolf was truly wondrous and, for Holly, it was nothing less than an event as miraculous as when she first saw the face in the pine tree. Calmly, the huge wolf slowly padded silently forward towards Holly. She held her breath but bravely stood her ground and still thought words of respect, friendship and love. Then, in response to the wolf moving nearer, she involuntarily held out her right hand as she had done to the wolf cub earlier that day.

I want to be your friend, thought Holly repeatedly, as the wolf stood completely still in front of her not even blinking his fierce amber eyes. Some urge deep within her caused Holly to raise her hand and touch the wolf on the side of its neck. She touched there because she wasn't quite tall enough to reach the top of the wolf's head easily. At the first touch of her hand, the wolf lowered his huge head and Holly moved her hand to rest in the thick fur.

When Holly touched the top of the wolf's head, it almost felt like another hand, a warm hand, was on top of hers gently pushing her fingers through the thick rough outer coat into the dense hair of the warm soft undercoat. As her hand moved, a surge of pure energy ran through her body, from the fingertips of her hand to the ends of her toes. No longer did her whole body feel as cold, and she felt strong and almost invincible, she felt she had gained some of the strength of the wolf, strength enough to go on and complete her task.

Holly stood very still with her hand warmly hidden in the thick coat of the grey wolf but, even when buried in the thick hair, she still had the sensation another hand, with the lightest of touches, was resting on her hand and holding it in place. She had no idea how long she had been like that when she suddenly remembered she'd left Pinofita behind in the tree hollow. Slowly, to avoid spooking the wolf, Holly removed her hand and, with that movement, lost the feeling of the other hand on hers. Whilst still looking into the amber eyes that had now lost their glint of anger, she thought, *Thank you my friend. Please don't go.*

The wolf remained still in the fast-falling snow, but his great head seemed to nod, ever so slightly but it was still a nod. Holly smiled a radiant smile believing he had understood, which meant she had talked to him with her mind!

Holly quickly turned and walked back to the tree hollow where her small friend stood on the snowy ground waiting for her. As Holly reached down to pick Pinofita up, her eyes were drawn to some huge animal tracks in the snow in the tree hollow. They were not her footprints nor were they the paw prints of the wolves. Some other large animal had been here before them. Holly thought she must have missed seeing them since she had been so tired when they first entered the tree hollow and thought nothing more about it, but that small, interesting piece of information was now stored somewhere in her head, even though she had stopped thinking about it for now.

ABOUT A DAY and half's walk to the north of where Holly, Pinofita and the wolf pack were getting ready to leave the hollow tree, the hooded men sent to lay the ambush had finished their preparations. They stood back and, from the rocky side of the clearing, surveyed the area. They all shared a cruel smile with each other since there was no obvious sign of the trap they had carefully laid between a small group of saplings in the middle. It looked a perfectly normal clearing with a thicket on one side and rocks on the other. They turned and made their way to the small camp they had created within the rocks and sat down to eat some very late supper. All they had to do now was to wait. Wait for the single person to come their way to certain capture and then a very uncertain future once back at the castle to stand before the warlord and that vile floating red thing that they all detested but also feared.

HOLLY, WITH PINOFITA safely in her hood, walked slowly back out into the snow towards the huge grey wolf, who had stayed exactly where she had left him. This time Holly did not feel as nervous as she had the first time she had approached the pack leader. Standing before him, once again she put her hand on his neck and thought.

Thank you, I hope you understand we did not harm the cub and we would never try and harm you. We will go back to our hollow tree now and finish the night sleeping before we continue north in the morning to finish the task we have started. So goodbye.

Holly had barely finished her thoughts when the wolf before her dropped his huge body into a lying position in the snow. Holly was taken aback, she didn't know what this meant, and she didn't know what to do.

'Climb on his back,' a familiar small voice in her ear whispered, 'he will help us go north much quicker than we could walk, and that will save us lots of time.'

'Are you sure?' said an incredulous Holly, 'climb onto this wolf and ride him?'

'Yes, do it now,' replied Pinofita.

With her heart beating like mad, Holly moved to the side of the wolf and, holding onto a handful of very thick grey coat, she pulled herself up and, kicking one leg over his back, she straddled the wolf.

Immediately the huge grey wolf straightened his

front legs to sit up, nearly throwing Holly and Pinofita off his back, causing Holly to squeal with a combination of laughter and terror. Holly managed to hold on by gripping the handful of grey coat even more firmly and then, as the wolf raised itself onto its back legs, it stood tall and proud on all four paws making it easier for Holly to get a good grip and steady herself.

The wolf turned its head to look at Holly with amber eyes that were now not so scary. Then it slowly turned and, leaving the rest of the pack, it began to trot north through the driving snow, the forest and the dark, freezing night. When the wolf sensed Holly had a secure hold, he increased his speed to that steady wolf lope that he could keep up for hours, and that ate up the miles so quickly, so much faster than a child with a mouse in her hood could walk and so much faster than a killing storm could travel!

THE EVIL SPIRIT had been floating in front of the warlord listening to the warlord talk about what he was going to do to that nuisance of a child. The evil one cared not whether the child was kept as a slave in the castle or staked out in the high forest as a meal for the wolves, or whatever other horrible fate the warlord could think of. The evil spirit didn't even think any of these terrible fates would happen since she was now confident this second night under the killing storm would see the end of the child. Once that happened, she would be free from the bonds of the wish and could do whatever her evil senses led her to do.

As the warlord sat down heavily in his chair, he looked at the red evil spirit swirling in front of him and growled 'So, when she is in my power and I have decided her fate, I suppose that is my wish complete and you will be free?'

He had expected the spirit to nod its empty hood in agreement, but what happened caused his cruel face to grimace in amazement and then, when he realised the implications for him, his face became contorted with fear!

Instead of nodding its cape hood to confirm it would be free, the red evil spirit suddenly writhed as though in agony. It began spinning and twisting like it was trying to overcome a terrible and sudden pain. The swirling red mist doubled over and then spun, it was out of control. The warlord looked on in horror for he knew then that the red storm was part of the essence of the evil spirit and the spirit could feel the storm and what affected the storm. Something had gone wrong with the killing storm spell.

HOLLY, WITH PINOFITA clinging on in her cape hood, was having the time of her life. The trees and snow seemed to fly by as the huge grey wolf loped north through the forest. She could feel the power of his body as she squeezed her legs into his sides and through her fingers as she clung on tighter than ever to his thick coat. It was exhilarating and breathtaking.

They were travelling north so quickly and, as the night and the distance went by, she realised just how far she would have had to walk, and the awful doubt crept into her mind that she might not have been able to do it. With a shiver for what that would have meant for her and Pinofita, she clung on and looked at the snowflakes rushing towards them. Interestingly, Holly also noticed the snowstorm was now weaker than it had been at the hollow tree. The falling snow was now so much lighter. They seemed to be leaving the storm behind!

And that was the problem with the evil spirit. The storm had lost its target child and it couldn't follow as quickly as Holly was now travelling. Such was the speed that Holly had escaped the centre of the killing storm, it was causing the storm to lurch and twist which, in turn, made the evil spirit do the same. The warlord didn't need to be told what had happened; he knew from what the spirit had told him before. Without any further hesitation he leapt out of his chair and ran as fast as he could up to the top of the wooden tower.

When he reached the top level, he looked south to where the red killing storm ought to be hanging over the forest and over the child. What he saw now filled him with horror and, although he didn't want to admit it, a growing sense of fear. The storm was no longer stationary over one spot in the forest. It was pulsing and, to his mind, writhing like it was in agony as it tried to find its target. It also looked much paler and smaller.

What the warlord didn't know was that every time the killing storm had to change direction, it lost some of its force and, as it did, so did the evil spirit. If he had known that he would have been even more doubtful of the spell's ability to rid him of the child.

As the warlord entered the great hall, the red spirit, which was a lot paler than before, was now circling high above the flagstone floor. He ignored it and went to his chair, his only comfort being that he had already sent his men into the forest to lay the ambush. As his cruel mind turned over the facts, he couldn't quite understand what exactly had made the storm, and the spirit, react as they had. Obviously, it concerned the girl, but what had she done to make this happen?

How could she, a young girl, have a way of avoiding a killing storm? It made no sense to him but, as he retired to his bed for the night, the last disturbing thought he had before he fell into a restless sleep was, where was she now?

WITH HIS WARM cloak wrapped around him, Edmund sat miserably at the front of his snow covered den and looked out in the early morning light. He had spent another day and night in the forest and now he really wanted to go back to the village. He had not slept well; in fact, he had hardly slept at all, since he was cold, uncomfortable and hungry. He could see the snow had almost stopped falling and, in fact, it seemed to be not so deep, so getting out today was a possibility.

As he looked through the lightly falling snow, he gazed across the snow covered clearing towards the dark woods on the far side. It was at that exact moment he caught sight of something moving through the trees. What he saw made him hold his breath and his heart to skip a beat, something that, in the first moments of recognition, changed his life completely. What he had understood and believed about myths and legends in his years growing up and living in the forest, was now turned on its head, as everything he thought he knew and understood was now called into question.

Across the far side of the clearing and racing through the trees heading north, he saw a figure with a green cape billowing out behind, sitting astride a huge grey wolf!

In that moment, the thought that rang clear as a bell in his mind was that the legend he had been told as a boy was true.

The forest was rising up to fight the evil attacking it. This was exciting, extraordinary news that he had to share with all the folk in the village. Without even stopping to collect what little food was left in the den, he jumped up and began to run through the snow back to the village, his mind racing with possibilities and his heart filled with hope.

37

THE WOBBLY STORM

A S DAWN BROKE over the village, Eryk was already up and dressed and standing outside looking up at the sky to the north. He could not quite believe what he was seeing. No more snow had fallen overnight; in fact the snow that had been lying on the ground was virtually all melted and gone, as had the snow that had only recently blanketed every roof in the village. That was all encouraging to see but, what really held his attention, was the red storm.

He shouted for his wife to join him. Within moments a very worried Boda, wrapped in a warm shawl, came out of the door in answer to his call.

'What's the matter?' she cried, 'Is it Holly?'

'In a way, yes,' he said, 'And I think it's good news!'

His wife grabbed his arm whilst frantically looking around as if her daughter must have returned. 'What's good news? Where?'

He raised the arm she wasn't holding and pointed to the red storm in the sky.

'The storm. Look at it, what do you see?'

She stared up at the storm and, after a moment, declared 'It's still red but not as red as it was and it's further away than before and wobbling.'

'Yes, you could say that,' grinned her husband, 'I don't really know which word to use to describe it, but I think it's … hesitating!'

At that moment, the storm seemed to move first one way and then another across the sky almost as if it didn't know which way to go.

'Hesitating?' Boda queried, 'Why would it hesitate?'

'I think that might be the good news,' said Eryk. 'To me, that means, if it is following Holly, it doesn't know where she is, she's escaped from it!'

'Oh, please let it be that,' gasped Boda, 'Please let her escape and come home.'

'She won't do that,' said Eryk gently, 'She knows if she comes home, the storm follows and we all suffer.'

'What will she do then?' Then Boda answered her own question. 'She will still try to find and destroy the warlord and the storm, won't she?'

Eryk turned to her, hugging her to his chest. 'The thought of it terrifies me, too. It would be so much better to know she wasn't alone out there with only Pinofita to help her.'

THE HUGE GREY wolf had run tirelessly all through the night with the two small adventurers on his broad back. After the dawn had come and a weak sun rose above them, Holly could see the snow had stopped, in fact there was very little snow lying on the forest floor. Her heart skipped a beat as she realised that at last they were clear of the red storm, the snow and the freezing cold.

Holly had no way of knowing how far they had travelled, or indeed how far they still had to go. What she did know was that they were so much closer to the warlord now than her walking speed could have brought them in the same time. This made her feel good and the hope that they might succeed in their task began to grow again inside her, like the warmth of a sunbeam on a hot summer's day.

Holly couldn't remember sleeping during the night, but she thought she must have done at some stage because she didn't feel tired. There again, how could she have slept whilst riding the wolf? This question kept going round in her head but, no easy answer came, so she just accepted that not feeling tired was another thing she didn't understand, as she didn't quite understand how, at that very moment, she could be riding a huge grey wolf!

The pace of the wolf slowed and then, as it reached a large outcrop of dark-coloured rocks rising out of the forest floor, the wolf stopped and lay down.

Holly took this as a sign that she was to dismount, which she did. Once her feet were firmly on the ground, she staggered forwards a few strides – her legs were stiff! Then she turned to face the wolf. He climbed to his feet and as Holly lifted her face to look at his, she thought the wolf didn't look so fierce as he had done when she had first seen him in front of the tree hollow. She smiled and, in her mind, thanked him for his kindness in helping them and bringing them this far north.

Next to her ear a small voice whispered, 'Holly, can you please lower your hood for me?'

Without replying or taking her eyes off the huge grey face in front of her, Holly slowly raised both arms and gently pushed her cape hood back.

With her hood fully back, Pinofita was now totally visible as he sat quite still on her left shoulder. Holly was not sure what might happen next, so she held her breath, stayed silent and waited.

It wasn't what Holly expected but, when it did happen, it made her whole body tingle again with the same feeling she'd had when the fingers of the figure from the pine tree had brushed her hand. The wolf slowly moved his head forward and his nose gently touched the nose of Pinofita, who had stood on his back legs as high as he could to meet the wolf's greeting.

Holly was thrilled. She was even more thrilled when the wolf drew back and then bowed his head. Realising what he was doing Holly bowed her head so, when contact was made, it was forehead to forehead, a contact made between friends, as both a greeting and a farewell.

Without a backwards glance the huge grey wolf turned and loped off through the trees to rejoin his pack. Holly watched him go and then she lowered the right hand that had been waving a fond but sad and incredulous goodbye. Again, it was the familiar small voice in her ear that brought her back from her daydreaming.

'Time to go Holly. There's lots of daylight left so let's

make the most of it and let's find some berries or seeds if we can, because I'm starving!'

Smiling, Holly pulled her cape up over her head and looked around her. Then, after a moment considering which way to go, she made up her mind and they set off along a path that she felt certain would eventually take them to the castle.

What they both didn't know was that this same route would also take them to a clearing with a thicket of bushes on one side and a series of rocks strewn on the other and an invitingly easy path right through the middle of it!

ALL MORNING THE warlord had paced the highest level of the wooden tower. His anger was directed towards the evil red spirit who had promised to fulfill his one wish by creating a killing storm to rid him of the girl, but that hadn't worked yet, and he wasn't sure it ever would.

The warlord didn't even bother to try and ask any more questions of the evil red spirit who was now looking paler than ever and quite a bit smaller than it had been. All morning the evil one did nothing except hover and writhe near the ceiling in the great hall and, occasionally, utter a hollow moan like a thin wind blowing through leafless branches.

It was clear the storm had lost the child as that same child had somehow raced through the night getting ever closer to the castle, and causing the evil one agonies that grew ever stronger. Even in its agony, the evil spirit thought about, but could still not fathom out who, or what, was helping the child.

One thing was certain, whatever it was, it was incredibly powerful and something to be feared.

38

THE NET CLOSES

ALL MORNING EDMUND had run like he had never run before. The path he followed he knew well and, if he could keep his current pace up, he thought he might reach the village before nightfall or just afterwards. He was elated by the sight he had witnessed of the figure in green riding on a huge grey wolf, just as the legend had said. Except now he could tell people it wasn't a legend; it was the truth, he had seen it! It was that feeling of elation that gave strength to his legs to enable him to keep running hour after hour. As he ran, he let his mind turn over the question of who the green figure on the wolf was, could it possibly be human or was it something else?

FEELING STRONGER AND more confident than she had since the day she'd left the holly sprig for her parents and closed the door on her home, Holly walked as quickly as she could through the forest. The snow on the ground was much thinner here, so progress was much quicker. The small travellers had no idea how much further they had to go until they reached the castle so all they could do was keep going and to trust that Holly instinctively knew the right path to take.

After walking most of the morning, with very little talking so Holly could conserve her energy, the trees eventually began to thin out. The space ahead wasn't a huge clearing, more of a glade really, but it had three very distinct features that made Holly pause in the cover of the trees to look carefully ahead.

On her left side she could see a line of thorn thickets that were dark and very bushy. There were a few places in the thickets where, if you really wanted to, you could crawl into the spaces under and between the bushes. Holly had no intention of crawling into any of the dark spaces, of course.

To Holly's right there was a tumble of large rocks that seemed to make a solid wall on that side of the clearing. Although, she saw shadows that made her think that there was space between the larger rocks that might be big enough to allow a person to pass between.

Holly studied the clearing one last time, her sharp eyes scanning to every feature, including the open centre of the clearing where only a few saplings grew. She noticed three or four of the saplings were slightly bent over but she thought that was just because the snow that had rested on them had become too heavy, causing them to bend.

She couldn't say why, but she was hesitant to leave the cover of the trees and enter the clearing. She felt that her path north lay straight through the centre of the clearing but, for some reason, some new instinct within her, she didn't trust that it was safe.

'What do you sense?' asked a cautious little voice in her ear. Interestingly Pinofita hadn't said 'see' or 'feel'. He'd used the word 'sensed.' He used that word because that was exactly what had struck him when he too had first seen the clearing through the trees. He'd sensed something wasn't quite right. He could also feel and see that Holly was very concerned.

'I'm not sure,' came her reply, 'nothing definite.'

'Is there another way around and then somehow we get back onto the path we were following?' asked her friend.

'I don't know. I just know the path across the centre is the way we need to go,' replied Holly.

Several minutes passed and still Holly stood perfectly motionless within the trees, not moving forward, but constantly looking from left to right and then back again. All the time she was doing that, a pair of cold blue eyes, shrouded in a hood, watched her from behind one of the rocks far to her right, a rock that wasn't really near the open part of the clearing, but it had a good view of the path through the trees where Holly and Pinofita now stood.

As planned, the lookout (because that was what this hooded man was) pulled on a long, thin piece of rope that was attached to the ankle of another hooded man completely hidden from Holly's view behind a large rock at the side of the clearing. Neither Holly nor Pinofita could see the thin rope as it was pulled, but the man who was attached to it felt the gentle tug on his ankle and, in response, gripped his spear even tighter. The person they had been sent to capture had been seen – it wouldn't be long now, he thought, until whoever it was was trapped and caught!

At long last Holly made her decision and whispered, 'I've decided to cross the clearing but I'm not going straight across. I can't say exactly what is wrong, but I'd be happier going round the edge to get to the other side.'

'Understood, but which side are you going to keep to, the thicket side or the rocks?' asked her little friend.

'I think the rocks side,' said Holly slowly. 'If anything happens, then we can scramble through the rocks, whereas that thicket looks too dense and strong to push our way through.'

'Fine by me,' encouraged the small voice by her ear.

Taking a deep breath Holly stepped forward and, out of the shelter of the trees, slowly made her way to the start of the rocks on the right side of the clearing.

'Bother!' exclaimed the hooded lookout under his breath, as he saw Holly begin to walk to the side of the clearing. She wasn't supposed to do that. Their ambush plan meant she had to walk through the middle of the clearing, not along one of the sides. Now he wasn't sure what to do.

Holly, with a very alert Pinofita in her hood, made her way one careful step at a time along the rocky side. Her eyes were looking everywhere, and she kept her ears open for the smallest noise that would alert her to any danger, braced and ready to run for safety in the trees.

The lookout was still trying desperately to think what to do when he had what he considered a brilliant idea. Probably the best idea he had ever had. Without thinking any more, he took a firm grip of the thin rope and then, putting it over his shoulder, he pulled at the same time as running as fast as he could in the opposite direction to the way the rope was trailing. The result was most unexpected and its effect quite spectacular!

Holly and Pinofita were just creeping closer to the biggest boulder in the clearing when, without warning, there was a loud shout of shock and protest as a hooded man sort of fell out from behind the rock with arms outstretched. His spear flew from his grasp and then he disappeared, facedown but moving backwards behind the boulder, almost as if he was being dragged!

Holly shrieked in surprise and alarm, threw her arms up in the air and ran as fast as she could across the clearing through the saplings to get to the forest on the other side where their path to the north lay.

All was going well. The hooded man wasn't following and no other hooded men appeared. Holly was running as fast as she could and was now between the saplings when suddenly she, with Pinofita clinging on as best he could, was not running on the ground towards the trees on the other side anymore, they were both rushing upwards into the sky.

They were caught within a net! A net suspended by ropes on four bent over saplings that now released and straightened up very quickly, and in doing so pulled the net and Holly and Pinofita up into the air before closing tightly over them.

They had been captured.

HOLLY LOST ALL sense of direction and orientation as she hung upside down. She was swinging from side to side within the strong mesh confines of the net. She screamed her protest but no matter how hard she kicked her legs or punched with her arms, she couldn't escape the strong embrace of the net. She was trapped.

Her mind was racing. Why hadn't she seen the clues of the bent saplings as the real danger? From her upside-down position, she saw hooded figures with spears approaching from the rocks and her heart sank further, since she recognised who these men were. She'd seen them before in the camp at the top of the gully near her village. They were the warlord's men!

A cold wave of desolation swept over her.

'It's over' she whispered to herself, 'I've failed, so what will become of my parents, the village and me now?'

Her mind then flipped from thinking about her situation to that of her friend. Was he all right?'

'Pinofita,' she called anxiously, 'Are you still with me, are you safe?'

She got the same response she'd had back in the forest the night they ran from the warlord's tent, silence, nothing, he wasn't in her hood! Holly tried to turn to see if she could see Pinofita in her hood but the net restricted her movements so she couldn't turn her head enough. Tears welled up in her eyes as she called again and again, 'Pinofita, please answer me, please.' And each time she called she received the same stomach-churning silent reply.

He'd gone!

39

THE WARLORD'S CASTLE

AS THE FOUR hooded men gathered round the swinging net, they had a better look at the captive in their power.

'I don't believe it's possible,' said one gruff voice, 'It's her, that little girl with the pole who stabbed our master's foot.'

'What!' exclaimed another voice, *'She's* the attacking force the warlord told us to capture? A little girl!'

As one, the hooded men all began to laugh cruel nasty guffaws of loud laughter that echoed off the rocks and around the clearing. They began taunting the girl who was still swinging upside down in the net but who'd given up fretting for her friend for now and was looking back at them with gritted teeth and glowering eyes. Holly was frightened but she wasn't going to let these horrible men see that. She was looking for a way to escape and, if possible, somehow manage to finish her task.

As they continued to laugh, her captors pushed and pulled the net, causing Holly to swing and sway but they didn't do anything else that might have hurt her. Despite being pushed and pulled Holly ignored her upside-down swinging position and began to plan. She thought that as soon as they let her out of the net to walk her back to the castle, she might have a chance to break free and to escape. She promised herself, if that chance came, she'd take it no matter what she had to do.

The problem with that plan was that the men didn't take her out of the net. They just released the net from the saplings and, with it still firmly closed around her, put a long pole through the top side of the mesh and, with a man at each end of the pole, they carried her. She was furious but entirely helpless.

Once the other hunters had gathered up the few things left in their camp, the party of four happy and laughing hooded men, and one swaying, silent and furious girl, set off at a fast trot back to the castle. As they set off, one of the men who had gathered up the things from the camp, accidentally dropped a few items he'd just collected, bits of meat and stale bread but, he was so focused on getting back to the castle before nightfall, he didn't notice.

As they travelled north they talked about how pleased the warlord would be with them, and if they might receive a reward or some big surprise. In their greed to have a reward or surprise, what they didn't consider, is that some surprises are nice to get and some are not!

AS THE EVENING light cast long shadows through the trees, Edmund was becoming exhausted. He'd run all day and was amazed how far and fast he'd come but he still had some way to go and every bone in his body was aching and his muscles were screaming at him to stop. He was so tired he couldn't remember being this tired before. All he wanted to do was to rest somewhere – anywhere – and just close his eyes and sleep.

Whenever he'd felt like this earlier in the day, he always thought back to what he'd seen and how important it was for the village to know that they weren't alone as hope was now out here in the forest, riding on a huge grey wolf!

Now the image of the rider in his mind gave him extra energy to carry on running and, every time he thought of the green figure on the wolf, he seemed to feel a fresh breath of air on his face that gave him more energy to carry on through the forest back towards his village. What Edmund never saw was the face that appeared alongside him, gently blowing into his face and giving him the strength and courage to complete his exhausting task.

40

DIFFERENT
NIGHTMARES

PINOFITA SHOOK HIS head and then immediately regretted it, for on one side of his head was a lump, a very sore and tender lump. A lump caused by his head hitting a small rock when he had been thrown out of Holly's hood and through the mesh of the encircling net onto the rough ground. He had been knocked out and had no way of knowing for how long he had been unconscious.

He slowly sat up and looked around for any sign of Holly or the hunters. He saw nothing but saplings, a thicket and lots of rocks. He had never felt so alone since the night he was in the warlord's tent. He had always been with his friend Holly and that's where he wanted to be now, not here on his own in the forest, not knowing where his friend was or what was happening to her.

Looking around where he sat, he could make out lots of footprints in the thin layer of snow, but it was a real mess of jumbled up prints. He then slowly walked around the area of trampled snow and could make out a series of footprints in a more orderly pattern heading out of the clearing, in the direction Holly had said she would have followed once they had crossed the clearing.

'That must be the way they have gone, and that must also be the way to the castle,' he said aloud to himself.

His instinct was to help Holly, to protect her but, as a tiny mouse, he knew he couldn't travel very far or very fast to catch up with the armed men who had taken Holly prisoner. Pinofita thought if he were bigger, he could travel much faster and maybe even catch them up and free Holly.

In his desperation he squeaked, 'Be bigger, be bigger.'

He waited but nothing happened. Then he tried again and again and again, squeaking even louder than before with each attempt.

Try as he might, Pinofita could not make himself big and, as he couldn't do that, he knew he couldn't run after Holly and rescue her. Slowly he hung his sore head in defeat.

With a big sigh, he looked up to the darkening sky and saw that night was coming soon, so he felt what he should do was to hide somewhere, rest and then, at first morning light, head off to find Holly following along the tracks he had seen leaving the clearing heading north. With a heavy heart, Pinofita crawled under one of the big bushes and found a dry patch of leaves near the base of the bush and, wrapping his tail around him, curled up to rest hoping his head didn't hurt so much in the morning. He tried not to think of his friend, but strange images crept into his dreams of Holly being chased by hooded men and having to struggle and fight to save her life. Pinofita twitched and squeaked all night, it was a bad dream.

AS PINOFITA WAS settling down to his night of bad dreams under the bush, Holly was living a nightmare of her own. Trapped in the swaying net, all sorts of dark thoughts were creeping into her mind about what might have happened to her little friend Pinofita, but she forced herself to concentrate.

Escape from the net was, she decided, unlikely. The net was made of some very strong material and her fingers could not break it or snap it. No matter what she did, it held firm and continued to hold her a prisoner. Now the forest they were travelling through was losing its trees and bushes and becoming a blackened space of tree stumps and devoid of other life. It was so horrible that just looking at it made Holly shudder.

Then, ahead of her, she saw what she had set out on this journey to find – the warlord's castle.

It rose out of the blackened cleared forest floor and was a size and height the like of which Holly had never seen before. To her it was ugly, massive and cold, and it certainly didn't look like a warm place to live – like her own cottage was.

As they covered the last few yards, the huge wooden gates swung open like the mouth of a giant and the four hooded men, and Holly, were all swallowed up by the impossibly large opening.

41

THE GREAT HALL

THE WARLORD WAS again in his great hall by a fire specially built up with extra logs, so the flames rose higher and roared louder than usual. For the first time in a long time he was happy, with a horrible grin of victory on his dark-veined face. Hovering high over the warlord in the rafters, the red evil spirit watched the source of her torment enter the hall. Once this girl was dealt with, she would be released from her obligation to the warlord, and free to go about her evil ways.

The four men who had captured Holly, together with the other remaining men who had now been called back from their guarding duties, marched down the length of the great hall. Holly was sitting in the net, suspended from the pole carried by two of her captors. She was still helpless and, to make matters worse, she was about to face the person she had set out to defeat; the huge, grinning warlord.

As she sat in her mesh prison, Holly looked around the large room she was in – in fact the largest room she had ever been in. She had never thought rooms could be this big. She focused first on the warlord, remembering him from the night she stabbed him in the foot with her sharpened pole, a memory that brought a hint of a smile to her face. Tonight, he looked even more frightening and ugly than she remembered. To his left she saw a small door that she thought might lead to a cupboard, in fact it was the door to the tower. To his right she could see two large wooden doors, probably leading to another part of this huge castle. There were no other ways to escape, and only one open window high up in the wall, much higher than she could ever reach.

The firelight played on the grim faces of the hunters who stood around her. As she turned her head, her eyes were drawn to the walls and the trophy heads of the many animals displayed there. Her heart sank. They shouldn't be there she thought, they should be running around and living their lives in their forest home.

Seeing the heads on the wall made Holly sad but it also did something else. It lit a fire of determination within her whole being; in her mind, in her body and in that part of her that had been awakened by Pinofita, the huge grey wolf and the lovely face with the green eyes. Deep within her, the special place some people call the soul.

Holly moved her gaze back to the warlord, her eyes glistening with pity for the animals on the wall but also glowing with a renewed determination to make him pay for this cruelty. If it was the last thing she did, she promised herself, she would finish what she had started.

It was at that moment Holly's gaze was drawn to something else in the room, something red tinged, swirling and hovering above the warlord's head.

What on earth is that? she thought, her body recoiling in horror at the inhuman shape writhing before her. It seemed to be looking at her, but from a dark recess in the red hood where a face should have been. *This is it,* thought Holly. *This is what caused the red storm.* But then she shivered at the thought of how she was ever going to make the warlord pay and get rid of this red thing.

SAFE WITHIN HIS castle, in his own great hall and supported by his remaining men and the evil spirit, the warlord was in control. He had the girl who had stabbed him in the foot and caused him so much pain and discomfort. He wanted to enjoy the moment of her capture and humiliation before he finally decided how he would dispose of her. Or, he thought, perhaps he might prolong her punishment by keeping her as a slave in the castle to do all the nasty horrible tasks none of the men enjoyed doing.

Feeling there was nothing to fear from the little girl, he commanded his men to let her free from the net and bring her to him. He stood with his back to the roaring fire and watched through his dark cruel eyes as the men holding the poles lowered the net to the flagstone floor. Carefully the two men opened the net and, with another hooded man pointing a sharp spear at Holly, they roughly grabbed her arms and pulled her up. Holly kicked her legs causing one leg to become entangled in the net. With one man firmly holding her arms, the other bent to untangle the net from her foot. As soon as she was free, she was dragged to stand in front of the warlord. The hunter kept a painful grip on her shoulder as his master approached.

'So,' grinned the warlord, 'I have the pleasure of your company again. It's so good to see you my dear.'

As his sarcastic words died away, the room was silent except for the crackle and spit of the burning logs. The trophy heads on the walls seemed to be looking down on the horrific scene with even more anguish than ever in their dark, sad eyes.

Holly said nothing. She stood very still just glaring up at him and waited for whatever was to happen next.

'No limp this time little girl?' sneered the warlord, 'And no sharp pointed pole either, I see.'

He stared down at Holly willing her to say something or better still, to break down in tears. Holly did neither of those things. She just remained standing very still and watched and waited.

Staring back at her, the warlord leaned down and slightly forward so she could see the rising anger in his eyes set within his dark-veined and bearded face.

'You have been the cause of much pain and disappointment to me. You are a witch who managed to somehow fight off my hounds in the tent and caused it to burn down. You …'

Holly didn't hear what he said next. Her mind was now whirling with what she had just heard.

The warlord thought that she had fought with the

dogs in the burning tent with some powers she had conjured as a witch! Impossible. She was in the forest when the dogs were fighting, and the tent burned. There was only Pinofita ...

Pinofita? she thought.

Her strange thoughts in her head were interrupted by the words she now heard from the huge, ugly man in front of her.

'So,' he said. 'How to rid myself of you? There are many ways to do that. I could throw you off the highest tower in the castle to the rocks below, or we could travel to the high northern forests and stake you out on the cold ground for the wolves to come and tear you apart. Or—'

On hearing those words Holly's face, which until now had been a picture of anger and defiance, broke into a small smile. She didn't think her friend, the huge grey leader of the wolf pack, would either harm her or allow any other wolf to tear her to bits.

This change in Holly's expression was spotted by the warlord, who couldn't understand it. Wolves were the animals he feared most and her reaction was unexpected. Once again, he felt that small trickle of unease run down his back.

The awkward silence in the room was broken by the warlord who snarled new words of hate down at the girl standing in front of him. 'Those fates are too good for you, over too quickly, so you don't suffer enough for what you have done to me. I have decided what I am going to do with you, and it is this.'

Hearing those words, all the hooded men leaned

forward to hear better what their master had decided as a punishment for someone they now considered as a young witch.

But before the warlord could pronounce his final sentence on Holly, he was distracted by the arrival of the red evil spirit. The red mist moved down from near the rafters to hover by his side.

'Be careful what you decide,' the cracked and hollow voice said. 'If you are not rid of the child, then the wish is not fulfilled and I would not be free as we agreed.'

The warlord glared into the deep dark recess of the red hood and answered. 'I don't care what we agreed. I'm going to do what I want to do with her, with your consent or not.'

The evil one swirled in anger and, again the hollow voice was heard, but this time it had the edge of a threat to it. 'Break our agreement and I will carry out your wish here and now and then be free.'

The atmosphere in the room had altered. The warlord was not sure he should bow to what the red spirit had said. If he did, he would lose all credibility with his men, who were now looking down and shuffling their feet. They were looking nervous. To give himself time to think the warlord turned away and reached down to pick up another log to throw onto the fire.

As he did, Holly realised the hand holding her shoulder was not gripping as tightly as it had been. The other hunters were fidgeting and distracted, and the warlord had turned away to face the fire.

This was her chance. Take it now or stay and learn whatever horrible fate the warlord had decided for her and then suffer it!

In that instant, she acted.

Turning her head, Holly quickly sank her teeth into the fingers holding her shoulder. He gave a short bellow of pain. As soon as she felt him jerk his hand away, Holly hurled herself at the warlord who was still bending over towards the fire, but now trying to look back to see what the scream was about. Holly's full weight hit him on the hip, and he staggered forward off balance. As her body cannoned into him, her hand came to rest on the hilt of his dagger so that, as he stumbled, the dagger came out of the sheath and stayed in her hand.

Everybody moved then. The red spirit rose to be above the commotion and, with its talon-like nails, it opened the swirling folds of the red mist to reveal the pulsing red mass that was the source of its evil power. The bony fingers went to seize the repulsive red mass to fashion another spell!

Holly had to duck as several hunters lunged towards her all at once. She didn't wait to see what anyone else was doing. Diving under the outstretched hands of another hooded man, she ran towards the double doors she had seen when she first entered the great hall and, turning the handle of one of the doors, pushed against it with all her might. She had hoped to find a corridor behind the door, one she could run down and then hopefully escape from this horrible place.

But it wasn't a corridor. It was a dark and musty room!

As Holly struggled to close the door, she heard the angry shout of the warlord.

'Get her back here from out of that room. I've had

enough of her she has to go, NOW!'

To accompany his shouted command, the warlord flung a burning log from the fire in Holly's direction. It didn't hit Holly, but it did hit the doorframe with a flurry of sparks before rolling, still burning, into the room. She leapt back, frantically brushing the sparks from her clothes. The log was still smouldering, throwing a little light into the darkness.

With a sinking feeling in her tummy, Holly realised the door did not have a lock or a bar she could put across. She was trapped and, in a moment, she would be their captive again. Then the weight of the dagger in her hand registered in her mind and immediately she knew what she could do to prevent her capture – for at least a few moments more.

Bending down, Holly swiftly jammed the blade of the dagger under the door even as there was a thump of weight against it as the first of the hunters thrust their shoulders against it.

There was another awful crash against the wood. The door and the dagger began to move inwards a little.

The metal hilt of the dagger made a horrendous scratching, scraping noise as it was pushed over the stone flags. Then the hilt became wedged in one of the cracks between the flag stones and the door jammed tight, with the door opening too small for a man to squeeze through to the gloomy interior where a frightened Holly stood.

The noise in the great hall increased, as the warlord shouted ever more instructions to his men. More of the men came to push against the door and, the dagger hilt groaned but held firm, for now. Realising she had to find a way to shore up the shuddering door, Holly slowly backed away from it and into the darkness of the room.

She hadn't taken more than eight steps back when she gasped aloud as something touched her back. She was up against something that was cold and hard and unmovable. After her sharp intake of breath, Holly paused to gather her courage and then whipped around to face whatever she had bumped into. It was not anything she could possibly have imagined in her wildest dreams or nightmares!

As she turned, the weak light from the burning log allowed her widening eyes to see a huge red black stag standing motionless in the centre of the room. It was not alive. It was another awful trophy. For some reason Holly was not afraid; she was more angry than afraid, that such a wonderful creature had suffered this fate. Looking up, she could see the proud head and the massive rack of antlers the stag still possessed. Involuntarily she lifted her right hand to touch the cold nose and then to run her hand along the sleek neck.

Something very strange then happened.

The noise in the great hall seemed to all but disappear, all trace of fear fell away from Holly like leaves falling in the autumn winds and, in her mind, all she could see was a huge pine tree with a figure wreathed in a cape of leaves and flowers smiling down on her, and the kind voice she could hear was saying, 'Remember me to an old friend.'

With a jolt of understanding, Holly tapped her trouser pockets with her hands and, sure enough, there it was, the tube she had been given! Amazingly it was unbroken despite all the struggles and falls she'd had. As the noise of the shouting in the great hall returned and the hammering of bodies on the door, Holly ignored them, and quickly retrieved the tube.

Holding the stopper in one hand and the tube in the other, she pulled. The stopper came out easily and, knowing what she had to do, she reached up to tip the tube over the stag's body. Golden shimmering powder fell out of the phial onto the creature's broad back.

Holly looked into the dull dead eyes and whispered gently, 'A gift from an old friend who wanted to be remembered to you.'

Holly nearly tipped the whole contents over the stag, but as she stood back, she remembered the whole instruction she had heard at the pine tree when she was given the shimmering powder.

Use sparingly and remember me to an old friend.

Holly looked down at the crystal tube and saw there were a few grains left in it, but not many, not even a quarter full. She quickly replaced the stopper, put it back in her trouser pocket and looked up towards the stag. Holding her breath, she waited for it to happen, hoping beyond hope that it would happen again and in time.

42

THE GOLDEN LIGHT

THE NOISE FROM the great hall had reached a new height of anger and ferocity. It was now so much louder and more threatening than it had been. The door shuddered every time the men on the other side rammed their shoulders into it. The dagger hilt screeched and screamed, and it began to buckle and bend with the pressure from the men. The hunters shoved and pushed the door, whipped on by their master's cruel and angry yells.

The door was slowly but surely being pushed open.

Holly stood transfixed, rooted to the spot. All she could do was to stare at the slowly opening door and then two things happened simultaneously. At the very moment the dagger hilt shattered and finally gave way, and the door was pushed further open, from behind Holly, there came the rush of a bright searing golden light!

She gasped with both shock and relief, then immediately buried her head in her hands, covering her eyes from the burning bright light. Hope soared in her heart.

In the great hall there had been a cheer from the hooded men as the door finally gave way, only to be replaced by a deathly silence as the brightest beam of light they had ever seen shone out from the room where Holly was. The light was so intense they pulled their hoods over their heads and turned, ran or rolled away to get out of it. The evil one recoiled and groaned as the beam of pure, golden light shone out. The red spirit stopped trying to make another spell from the pulsing red mass, recognising there was now an even more powerful presence in the great hall than the little girl or herself. As quickly as it could, it rose through the ceiling rafters and carried on rising until it reached the top of the wooden tower where, in desperation, it looked to see where the killing storm was, and what remained of the spell that made it. It was too far away to return in time to help the evil one regain more power but it was still out there over the forest, but now paler and smaller and still frantically trying to find Holly.

When the intense bright light first burst into the great hall like an avenging fist, the warlord, standing at the back of his men, stood stock still like he had been frozen solid. His eyes, in his dark bearded face, bulged in surprise and his mouth fell wide open in disbelief and amazement.

'Not again' he muttered, 'First she fights three of my dogs in the tent and now this, whatever it is.'

As he continued to stare at the traumatic effect the light was having on his men, the trickle of icy fear he'd felt before returned to run quickly up and down his spine, as the one thought that echoed through his mind again and again was *she IS a witch!*

EVEN THOUGH HOLLY had witnessed the incredible effect of the shimmering powder once before, she still couldn't bring herself to believe it was happening again, but this time to save her!

Hope rose in her whole body and slowly she opened her eyes, peeping through her fingers that still covered her face, to see what the light had brought to life. If, on first seeing Pinofita come alive she had been amazed, what she felt now she had no words for. All she could do was gasp and stare.

The huge stag was still standing in the middle of the room, only now, as the inner light coming from his massive frame slowly faded away, his head turned to look down directly at Holly.

His red black coat shone with life and his dark eyes were now glistening with thanks to the small girl who stood next to him, and vengeance towards the men trying to get into his prison to harm her. His front legs stamped their cloven hooves on the cold flagstones beneath them and the wide, sharp-tipped antlers swayed and shone in the firelight. Turning away from Holly to face the great hall, the stag lowered his head and, without a sound other than that of his hooves on the flagstones, he charged out of his prison and into the throng of hooded men.

Holly stayed in the relative safety of the dark room but heard all the crashes, grunts and screams from the fight in the great hall. The hunters didn't actually put up much of a fight, so scared were they, when instead of a frightened girl coming out of the room, they were faced by a massive animal they had thought long dead! An animal that now sought not only his freedom from this castle prison, but also, the freedom of the girl who had made it possible.

The hooded men tried as best they could to ward off the attack by the enraged stag but few of them had brought their spears, and hands alone were of no use whatsoever. Those with spears tried to both defend themselves and attack the stag, but the fear that gripped them hampered their efforts. They couldn't think straight to co-ordinate themselves so, as the stag charged them, they held their spears more like shields, which didn't really work at all.

Others ran for cover. One hid behind the warlord's chair and two of the hooded men ran to grab the net that had encaged Holly, in the belief they could snare the stag in the same way. They hadn't quite reached the net when, after several bounds, the stag caught up with them. With his mighty head lowered, the enraged animal ran into the nearest man and the antlers scooped the poor wretch up and then tossed him to the far wall, where he landed with a dull thud and lay there, stunned.

The second man abandoned the fight. Instead, he jumped over the net, which was still lying on the floor and, with arms outstretched and a desperate cry, he crashed through the doors and out of the hall. He ran as fast as he could down the wide stone corridor to the courtyard outside. He didn't care where he went just so long as the stag didn't follow.

What he had done though, was to show the stag the way out of the castle to the courtyard and then beyond the courtyard and to the forest and freedom.

The hunters usually fought under the loud commanding orders of their warlord but, tonight, his voice was silent. In fact the warlord, at the moment the stag erupted from the room and charged headlong into his men, could think of nothing other than saving his own skin. He did what all cowards do, he ran!

He ran for the safety of the spiral steps that led up to the wooden tower, steps so narrow the stag couldn't follow. With his mind reeling, the warlord could not believe what he had just seen. The stag, a victim of a hunt so long ago, was now in the great hall, alive, and fighting his hooded men. That confirmed it for the warlord, the little girl must be a witch! The warlord believed only a witch with black magic could do what he had just seen. He never thought for one moment that forces for good also wielded magical powers, white magic!

The hunters took cover, as best they could, or they too ran for their lives away from the avenging stag. Soon the great hall was empty other than some groaning wounded hooded men on the floor and a triumphant stag standing proud in the middle of the havoc it had caused. The stag, seeing no further challenge, turned and walked back towards what had been his prison. In the doorway, waiting for him, was Holly.

As the stag approached her, Holly stood with a pale face and just looked into his eyes, still not quite believing what had happened. The stag came right up to Holly and turned, then stood still by her side. Holly needed no further invitation. She reached up with both hands and, gripping the thick coat, she pulled herself up onto the stag's back. When she was straddling the huge animal, she held on tight with both hands and the stag ran across the great hall and out through the double doors, down the wide stone corridor, across the courtyard to the forest and freedom.

Then Holly saw with a jolt that the heavy gates in the high wooden stockade were barred and closed!

43

A RED KILLING SPEAR

THE WARLORD STOPPED with his foot on the seventh step of the spiral staircase. His pride made him stop.

'No!' he shouted, his voice echoing up the stone staircase. He knew he had to go back; he couldn't let what had happened go unanswered. He must regain control and now finally rid himself of the girl and the stag.

Slowly he stepped back down the stone stairs and cautiously peered through the doorway into the great hall. His men were either crouching in fear at various positions in the great hall or were lying groaning on the cold stone flagged floor clutching their injuries.

High on top of the wooden tower, the evil spirit's attention was drawn from the storm spell to the noise in the castle courtyard below, where the stag with the young girl on its back galloped into the courtyard and skidded to a halt in front of the barred gates.

Slowly the red spirit drew the swirls of its red body mist apart and bony fingers with cruel curved talon-like nails moved towards the red pulsing mass within. Here was the chance, it thought, to rid itself of the child and the stag and then be free of its obligation to the warlord. The bony fingers pulled a lump of the red pulsing mass free and began to shape it into another killing spell but, this time, the hollow voice chanted sounds that would make something sharp and terrible that would obliterate whatever, or whoever, it hit.

The warlord could see that the stag and the girl had left the great hall. He called to his men to rally themselves, grab whatever weapons they could and follow him to finish them both. There was a scrape of metal on stone as the hooded men picked themselves up, grabbed the weapon nearest to hand, and moved as quickly as they could to follow their master. Before they could leave the great hall, a shout echoed down the corridor. It was the hunter who had jumped over the net and fled earlier.

'They're trapped in the courtyard, master,' he yelled triumphantly, 'stopped by the gates.'

The warlord's dark-veined face split into a wide grin of revenge and he rallied the men around him with a shout of 'Forward men, follow me and let's finish this. They can't escape, we have them!'

HOLLY NEARLY FELL from the stag's back when it skidded to a halt in front of the barred gates. Clinging on she looked at the heavy wooden beam across the gates and knew she couldn't lift it. There was no other way out since the wooden stockade was too high for the stag to leap over and the tops of the wooden poles in the stockade were sharpened points. They were trapped.

The warlord and his men saw the stag paw the ground in frustration.

'Form a line,' yelled the warlord, 'Get your arrows ready to fire first and then spearmen be ready to charge.'

The men obeyed immediately with three of the men drawing their bowstrings taut and aiming their sharp arrows at the stag.

'Bring him down first and then the girl has no protector,' screamed a jubilant warlord.

Holly stared through the curve of the stag's antlers in horror at the three archers and their sharp arrows, not to mention the four other hooded men who levelled their sharp spears at her and her protector, ready to charge once the arrows had done their evil work.

Holly felt herself tense in anticipation of the imminent attack and, underneath her, she could feel the muscles of the stag twitching and bulging ready to charge, one last time.

The warlord raised his right arm in readiness to signal the attack. 'Get ready.'

His voice was huge as it reverberated around the courtyard. At that very moment, the stag reared up to gain momentum to increase the speed of his intended attack but neither the arrows were released nor did the stag charge.

As the warlord uttered those last words, a red sparkling streak of hate came hurtling down from the top of the wooden tower and exploded with a mighty crash causing a thick red mist to envelop the courtyard – a thick red mist filled with an explosion of wood!

The evil red spirit had created its spell but misjudged the angle from the top of the tower. So, instead of hitting the stag and the girl, the spell smashed into the wooden gates, causing chunks of flying wood to arc over the stag and Holly, and then to be flung into the warlord and his seven men.

When the mist dispersed, the warlord and his men were cowering on the ground, with their hands and arms over their heads. A few of them were looking very groggy having been stunned by the flying wooden chunks. The gates in the stockade that had been closed were no longer there and neither were Holly and the stag. Holly was sitting astride the stag gripping on tightly to its neck as it galloped away along the path towards the forest.

44

A STORY OF HOPE

AT MORE OR less that same time, an exhausted Edmund staggered into the village. He stopped at the first cottage he came to and banged on the door. There was no answer, so he banged again and again.

'Who's there at this time of night?' came a sleepy and grumpy voice.

'Ed, Edmund,' he stammered, so exhausted he could barely speak.

'Edmund? What are you doing out at this hour?' came the same voice but now the tone was not so sleepy but a bit more concerned.

'Good news,' called Edmund, 'I have good news.'

The door opened and a yellow torch light lit Edmund's face now beaming with a huge smile.

'Come in, come in,' said Tomas. Tomas was one of the crop tenders for the village and knew Edmund well. Edmund staggered into the small cottage and sat himself down on one of the two wooden stools by the rough table.

'So, what's this good news you have to tell? No, before

I hear that, d'you want a drink? You look like you need one.'

Edmund just nodded his acceptance and Tomas left the small room but, within seconds, came back with some water. Edmund gratefully drank it down in one go.

'Go on then, what's this good news?'

'You're not going to believe it!' he smiled.

'Course I ain't, if I don't know what it is, what is it?'

Edmund paused, enjoying the moment then he said 'The legend is true!'

'What legend? Stop talking in riddles and tell me straight.'

'The legend that, when the forest is threatened, a green figure will arise and come to the forest's rescue and riding on a huge wolf!'

'Ha, that old story! My folks used to tell that one as well. It's a story it's not the truth. It's meant to tease the children nothing more.'

Edmund grew serious and he leant forward and looked Tomas in the eye and spoke with his most earnest voice. 'I swear on my life that's what I saw. No story Tomas, just the honest truth, a green figure riding on a huge grey wolf. In fact, riding north to where the red storm came from, the red storm that is now getting smaller. I tell you that's what I saw, the legend is true!'

Tomas scratched his head and looked at Edmund but now with a look of growing respect in his eyes for what he had just heard. 'If what you say is really true, we need to go and tell Boda and Eryk immediately.'

'Why?' asked the weary runner.

'Well, their young daughter, Holly, went missing on

257

the first day after the storm started and, as you'd expect they are very, very worried about her. No one has been able to get outside the village. Perhaps you've seen a sign of where she went?'

'Holly, missing, oh no, she'd not stand a chance in that storm! I know I've been sheltering from it since I don't know when. I haven't seen any sign of her. I'm sorry.'

'Well, I think they'll want to hear this direct from you all the same. C'mon let's go and wake them up like you did to me.'

With that Tomas helped Edmund to his weary feet and, with his arm around his waist for support, he helped Edmund walk the short way to the cottage on the edge of the village, a cottage that was now in darkness. When they arrived at the door, Tomas banged on it to make sure the sleeping occupants would hear him. They did.

'Who's there?' came the sound of Eryk's sleepy voice.

'Tomas, and I've got Edmund with me, and he has something very interesting to tell you.'

There were sounds of footsteps within the cottage, then a small light appeared under the door as a torch was lit and, after a few more moments the door opened.

In the doorway stood Eryk with Boda beyond him. She was holding Eryk's other arm, and in her free hand, she clutched the small sprig of holly.

'Have you found Holly?' asked Boda with a sound of trembling excitement in her voice.

'Er, no that's not what Edmund here has to tell you. But what he does have to say is quite extraordinary.'

'Come in then and tell us what is so extraordinary,'

said Eryk with his eyes looking expectantly at Edmund.

The two visitors stepped inside the cottage and were immediately invited to sit down.

'No thank you, we just want to give you the news of what Edmund here has seen, and then we'll be off,' said Tomas quietly.

'That's fine,' said Boda her voice now with more than an edge of excitement to it. 'Please don't keep us waiting any longer, what do you have to tell us Edmund?'

Edmund looked at both Holly's parents and then began. 'As you know, I was out foraging in the forest when the red storm hit us. It was so bad I had to shelter for a couple of nights since it was too dangerous to travel home.'

'Yes, we gathered that when you weren't in the village,' said Boda, keen for Edmund to get to the detail of what he had to say. Eryk's gentle pressure on her arm told her to be patient and let Edmund tell his story.

'Sorry Edmund, please carry on.' Boda said softly.

'It was on the morning of the third day, early morning to be precise, and I was looking out of my den trying to decide if I could come home or if the storm was still too bad. That's when I saw it.'

'Saw what?' chorused Boda and Eryk.

'The legend that's what!' exclaimed a proud Edmund.

'What legend are you talking about?' Boda asked, her voice now sounding very impatient.

'Oh yes, sorry,' apologised Edmund. 'I saw a green figure, cape all billowing out behind, riding north on a huge grey wolf! That means the legend is true it's not a story to tease children with.'

Boda just stared at Edmund and didn't say a word. The first voice to break the silence was Eryk's. 'A green figure you say, with a cape billowing out behind and riding on a wolf, a huge grey wolf?'

Edmund just nodded.

'That's it!' exclaimed Eryk triumphantly, 'The sign we've been waiting for.'

The small group all looked at each other and then the silence was broken by Boda. 'Thank you so much Edmund, thank you for telling us.' With glistening eyes, she stepped forward and reaching up, she kissed Edmund on the cheek.

After the door was closed and Edmund had left to find the old man and spread the news further, Boda rushed to Eryk and hugged him; the tears running down both cheeks were now tears of joy. She so wanted to hear some good news about Holly, and this was the best news yet, in fact, the only really good news she had heard since Holly and Pinofita had left.

'Could it be true?' she asked Eryk.

He nodded as he too didn't trust himself to speak.

After a moment he gathered his emotions and whispered, 'It is just as the legend said – the forest is now rising up to fight whatever is threatening it.'

A little later Eryk and Boda each thinking things through in their own mind, having gone over what Edmund had said several times. Staring into the crackling fire, Eryk murmured 'But to ride on a wolf, that figure must have been small. A grown-up would be too big.'

And a few moments later, Boda added, 'Holly, she has a cape, a green cape doesn't she?'

IN THE COURTYARD, the warlord was screaming his anger at the red spirit. 'Why do that? We had them. It would all be over by now and you would be free, but it's not over and you're not free. Not until I'm rid of that witch.'

The evil one didn't respond. It had drifted down from the tower to hover in front of him. Now it just waited to see what the warlord would do or say next.

The warlord rounded on his men. 'Come on, we have to chase that stag and the child witch. They are not to get away. Go and fetch what weapons you can run with, so nothing too heavy, a torch for everyone and bring the two dogs we have left. They can follow the scent when we cannot see the tracks of the stag in the forest. They won't get that far so come on, hurry!'

The men did as they were commanded but, for once, they were unsure if they wanted the warlord as their leader anymore. Things had been going wrong recently, and they were getting hurt. It didn't feel right. Reluctantly, they began to prepare for the chase.

As the group gathered in the courtyard, the warlord counted only five hooded men and two dogs. The rest were lying injured and groaning on the ground. He was the sixth man in the group and was now armed with his favourite sword. The seventh member of the group hovered close to his shoulder and said nothing. Looking at the assembled men, the warlord thought they looked a sorry group and nothing like the force of men he had led when he first set out to destroy the village. That reminded him of the moment when he first met the little girl who, in fact, had turned out to be a little witch. His foot still throbbed sometimes. That thought made his face grimace and want to be rid of her as soon as possible. So, with that black thought in his mind, he shouted to the hooded men to follow him, and then he set off through the broken stockade and began to follow the clear tracks of the stag in the sparse, shallow snow as once again he headed south. Slightly above the warlord's shoulder, the red evil spirit easily kept pace with him.

THE STAG RAN as never before. He needed to get as far away from the castle as possible to try and give his rescuer the best chance of escape. Holly didn't know it, but the stag had already sensed his strength was beginning to fade. Ignoring the sensation, the brave beast continued to run south through the forest, the forest that had once been his forest, his home. As he ran through the trees, he felt elated with the feeling of the forest floor beneath his hooves again, and of being alive but it was a feeling that had only a few hours left before it finally ended.

Holly gripped tightly and lowered her head to make herself as small as possible. As she rode south, the horrors of the castle began to fade, only to be replaced by the terrible feeling of emptiness as, once again, her thoughts turned to her friend Pinofita. Where was he now, what had become of him, was he all right and would she ever see him again?

45

WAR PAINT

AFTER TWO HOURS of following, the sharp eyes of the warlord saw the hoof prints they were following though the thin covering of snow were now not regular. A sign he was weakening!

The warlord shouted this to his men who all smirked and, gritting their teeth, ran all the harder. Maybe their master was right after all, they would be successful, their prey was getting tired and they were closing in for the kill. It felt like the old times in these woods when they had hunted the red black deer before.

THE STRENGTH WAS finally ebbing from the muscles of the stag. He had run as far and as fast as he could, but now he was nearly finished. He ran stumbling for another few hundred yards then he slowed to a walk and finally stopped near an old, gnarled tree.

Holly, who had been aware for some time of the exhaustion setting in on her brave friend, patted his neck and then, kicking her leg over the stag's back, dismounted and stood in the snow next to him. Slowly she walked forward then turned to face the proud head with the wide antlers. She was about to raise her hand to stroke the stag's head when he moved first.

He slowly lowered his head so that Holly could lean in and let their foreheads touch, for a long, drawn-out moment. With his head bent forward, the stag's antlers seem to form a last protective circle around the small girl in a green cape standing in the snow in the middle of the vast forest.

It was their goodbye.

The stag raised its head, turned and walked slowly through the trees it had known as a fawn. Holly stood motionless and watched feeling lonelier with every faltering step the stag made that took him further away from her. Holly thought something was wrong with her eyes because now she couldn't see the stag properly. He seemed to be shielded from her sight by trees that somehow were now between him and her but there were no trees between his body and where she stood. The truth was, he was fading away, and, with that she could see through parts of him. The shimmering powder had done its work but now that power was ending and the last Holly saw of the stag were his antlers, proudly held high and glistening in the moonlight. Then they too were lost into the cold night air. At last he was free.

With one last lingering look towards where she had seen her rescuer, Holly sniffed, wiped her nose on her sleeve and then turned. She sensed which direction she needed to go in, and then, as fast as she could, she ran along her chosen path between the trees. As she ran, she had to keep looking down to avoid tripping over tree roots. On one such occasion she was looking down but saw tracks heading the way she was coming from as if someone had passed this way towards the castle. Then they disappeared where the snow had melted and then reappeared again where the snow still lay. They seemed to have come from the direction she was heading in so she followed them in reverse, not really thinking about who or what might have made them.

Not far behind her, the hunting party was suddenly called to a halt by the warlord. They were all glad of the rest, but the warlord hadn't called them to stop for a rest. He'd seen something in the snow.

'We've nearly caught them,' he cried in an excited voice, 'Look at the prints in the snow here.'

The hooded men, panting and very tired all crowded forward and there, in the snow, they could see the prints of the stag and a sudden flurry of prints from the small witch girl. Then the stag's hoof prints went one way and the child witch's footprints went another.

'That's it,' cried the warlord, 'She's on foot now, on her own, no protective stag to look after her and fight for her.'

'Where is the stag who was brought to life by some powerful magic?' whispered the cracked, hollow voice near the warlord. 'You had better make sure he isn't waiting to ambush you.'

The warlord thought about it and then nodded and

266

sent three of his men and the two dogs to follow the stag's prints. The other men grouped in a rough circle and pointed their weapons towards the trees around them, just in case.

The dogs, with their noses to the ground, pulled the men holding them along. The scent was so strong here. They were close. But after only a few strides, the prints seemed to evaporate from the snow and even the dogs stopped sniffing, because there was nothing there to sniff.

'You say the prints and the scent trail just disappeared?' the warlord said incredulously when they returned.

The hooded men nodded but kept their mouths shut, sometimes it was best to do that when you had just delivered bad news to the warlord!

'So did the stag climb a tree or fly away?' he yelled, starting to get angry about something he didn't understand. Too many things had happened recently that he didn't understand, and he didn't like that.

'I may have an answer,' whispered the evil one.

The warlord turned to face the hovering, swirling spirit and, looking directly into the dark recess of the hood, where the face should have been. 'Well?'

'The answer, I think, is the stag was brought back to life by magic, but the magic was weak, so the spell didn't last very long. That's why he has now disappeared, disappeared into thin air, gone!'

The warlord didn't have a reply but thought long and hard about this explanation since, as far-fetched as it was, there was some truth to what the evil one had said. It must have been magic that brought the stag to life and, if the witch child was the cause of that, and who else could there be? Her magic might be small like she was. Small child, small magic hence small length of time it would work, now that made sense to the warlord.

He seemed happy to accept the evil one's explanation and, after nodding agreement to the hovering red mist, he then rallied his men.

'Now for the last part, the stag has gone and the girl is on her own in the forest with no weapons, no protector, so she will be ours very soon. We can run faster than she can so let's go and catch her before dawn. But remember, do not kill her, take her alive. It has to be my punishment that rids me of her.'

The men grunted their acceptance of that last command and, as they were slightly revived by their rest, they then carried on running quickly after the small tracks in the snow.

HOLLY HAD RUN as fast as she could for as long as she could but, now she was beginning to tire and tire very quickly.

'Just to that big tree up ahead, now to the bushes on the left.' She gasped encouragingly to herself.

All through the next hour or so, Holly kept urging herself to keep going. Then the barking of the two dogs told her the hunt was nearly over. They were still some distance away, but her scent was strong enough to excite the two hunting hounds. Her eyes frantically searched the path behind her, and she groaned when she realised the warlord was now so close, too close!

Her mind went back to the horrors of the great hall the previous night, it must have been the previous night she thought since she could see the red and yellow streaks of dawn in the sky.

She did not want to return to that grim massive hall, and she certainly didn't want to find out what he was going to do to her when he eventually caught her again.

Without checking to see which path she was taking, she ran instinctively between the trees where the moonlight had now given way to the first weak rays of the sun.

The sound of the baying hounds grew louder and louder, the dogs and the hooded men were gaining on her.

She thought, 'Need to hide, need to hide, but where, where?'

With the sounds of shouts now adding to the excited howls of the dogs, Holly knew they might be able see her through the trees, but she hoped beyond hope they couldn't. What was going to make matters worse was that, ahead of her, the trees were thinning out so making it easier for them to follow her.

With the last of her strength Holly ran through the sparse area of trees before the clearing opened up to reveal a line of rocks on the left, a few saplings in the middle and, on the right, a thicket of thorn bushes.

A thicket too strong and dense to push through, but with lots of small dark spaces at the base of them. Good places to hide.

Holly threw herself on the ground at the base of the thicket where there was a space underneath and started to crawl under the dense vegetation. The sharp thorns on the bush scratched Holly's forehead and clung onto her cloak. Turning her body, Holly angrily tugged her cloak free with such force that, when it came free of the thorns, she fell face first into the soil that had been made into soft mud by the recent melting snow. She wiped her face with her hands and couldn't see that she had created stripes on her face, and she had blood running down slowly from the shallow cut to her forehead.

If she could have seen her reflection, she would have thought she was looking at some strong female warrior, with her face painted for battle, not a small girl with mud streaks and a bloodied cut on her face. However, age does not alter determination, and mud and blood are just like war paint!

She had barely freed herself and made it to the back of the space under the thicket when the dogs and the first of the men were running through the last of the trees and into the clearing.

PINOFITA WAS WOKEN by the excited barking of the dogs and the shouts of the hooded men as they entered the clearing. He stayed very still and very low to the ground which, for a small mouse, was easy to do. He wondered why there were now dogs, men and an evil looking red mist in the clearing where his friend Holly had been captured.

Looking closer, Pinofita saw something even more strange. When they reached the saplings in the centre of the clearing, the dogs began picking things up from the ground and eating them. The reason was they were famished; they hadn't been fed for two days and they had been running all night. They had found the bits of crispy meat and stale bread dropped by the hooded men as they packed up their camp once Holly was safely in the net, only yesterday afternoon.

'What!' exclaimed the warlord, 'She's not hiding in the open, what are they doing?'

He yelled at his men to put the dogs on the leash again but that proved more difficult than you might imagine. The dogs were running free and, with noses to the ground, they were searching for more food to eat, so they ignored the commands shouted by their handlers. In fact, it went from bad to worse; not only did the dogs ignore the shouted commands but they also ran from the clearing and into the rocks. The two handlers and two of the other hooded men followed and eventually found the dogs sniffing the ground where the ambush party had built their camp. However, it wasn't easy to catch the dogs as they ran about excitedly, hoping to find more food.

In the clearing near Pinofita, the warlord was ordering his remaining hooded man to begin searching the bushes. When the hunter started to peer under the thickets and push his spear into the dense leaf cover, the warlord watched him, his hand on his sword hilt, ready for any surprise the young girl witch might try this time. While watching the hooded man search, the warlord became aware of the evil red spirit looking towards bushes near the far end of the line of thickets, not where the man near him was searching. The warlord dismissed this observation and went back to watching his man.

Pinofita focused on only one detail that seemed particularly important. The warlord had said they were hunting someone. A girl. Holly!

His hair bristled as he began moving towards where the warlord stood, keeping himself under the protective branches of the thicket. Creeping along in such a small space would be difficult for any human, even a small child but he wasn't. He was a small, furry brown mouse but a mouse that was getting angrier, the closer he got to the warlord.

The hunter with the spear who was searching the thicket pushed his spear into a large bush and pulled the spear to one side so hoping to see into the middle. Up until then all he had seen had been branches and leaves, no sign of the witch. As he moved the spear to the side this time, he came face to face with a face streaked with mud and blood staring back at him. Shocked he leapt back and shouted, 'In here – the witch, she's in here!'

The warlord raised a fist in a triumphant punch into the air and whooped with delight. They had her, no stag to magically come to life and save her this time, she was his.

The men in the rocks heard the shout and turned and ran back towards their master, who was now shouting more orders.

'All you men, weapons ready and form a semi-circle in front of this bush. Make sure she doesn't escape and where are those dogs?'

The men began forming the semi-circle and one of the dogs came bounding out of the rocks and returned to his handler who just held him by the scruff of the neck ready to send the animal into the bush to flush out the witch.

The warlord waited, savouring the moment of victory,

his moment of victory. He wanted all his men to enjoy this success, since he had felt his power over them had been slipping in the past few days. Victory now would regain their respect and loyalty to him. As he looked around, one thing was missing from the semi-circle, the evil red spirit.

The red spirit was peering about, distracted by something else.

The warlord raised his arm and yelled, 'Get ready to send the dog in.'

At that very same moment, the red evil spirit raised an arm and pointed with a bony finger at the bush to the left of the bush Holly was hiding in.

'There, THAT bush, something is coming out of that bush, defend yourselves!' screeched the cracked hollow voice.

46

THE TRUTH REVEALED

'NEVER LOSE HOPE for without hope all is darkness and despair.'

The remembered words echoed around Holly's head and from somewhere deep inside, she felt an inner strength grow. She looked up to stare at the men who confronted her, her narrowed eyes defiant once more, and a burning determination rose in her whole body to fight for as long as she could, with whatever she could.

What Holly saw as her head lifted was not what she expected. The semi-circle of men were now turning to the side of her and pointing their weapons in a slightly different direction. The dog began to howl with terror, and through the bushes to her right, she could see something. Something big, something that seemed to grow even bigger as she looked at it.

Slowly and menacingly the large shape moved out of the shadows of the thicket. Involuntarily, Holly drew back as far as she could from this new thing that had appeared out of the forest. As the shape moved slowly nearer, the semi-circle of hooded hunters stepped back.

The dog eventually broke loose from its handler and ran howling back into the forest and the red evil spirit slowly rose higher, out of harm's way.

Holly couldn't believe her eyes for, in front of the thicket where she crouched, she could see a huge brown creature with strong claws, twitching whiskers, pink ears laid back, a lashing tail, fearsome red burning eyes and a pink nose wrinkled up in a snarl that revealed two huge white teeth. The gigantic Pinofita looked at Holly and then turned and stood defiantly between her and the armed group, challenging them and ready to defend his friend to the death.

For Holly time stood still. Her mind was racing, having just seen the change in what she believed to be her Pinofita. Then pieces of the jigsaw of the recent past began to emerge from her memory and fall into place.

Firstly, the unknown creature that had fought with the three hunting dogs in the warlord's tent. There was no other explanation, he must be the creature that fought and defeated the dogs.

Then the strange rock she had passed when she ran back to save her friend. She'd always thought there hadn't been a tree root there, and now she could see Pinofita's muscular tail swishing on the other side of the bush, she nodded her head and knew the truth of her doubt.

She recalled when she was so cold and exhausted in the snow and dreamed of a freezing river that carried her away, and then her hand had grabbed the grass, the warm grass. Grass that had enveloped her whole body and kept her warm all night saving her life.

And, in the morning, the snow den they had made

seemed so much wider and deeper than she had dug with her hands. Pinofita again!

And when the wolf pack came for their cub, she had seen huge footprints in the snow when she returned for Pinofita. Had he helped calm the wolf and, in some way asked the wolf to help them? He must have because, why else would he have revealed himself to the wolf, and for the huge grey wolf to touch noses with him, as friends, just before the wolf left them?

Finally, just now, coming to her rescue in the same clearing where she had lost him as the net ensnared them but looking like nothing she had ever seen before. Could it really be, she thought, this is why the lovely figure in the green cloak of leaves and flowers gave me the shimmering powder on my birthday, so Pinofita would come to life, to help me now to defeat this evil in the forest?

Her mind was in a whirl, but it was now made up; her determination to succeed was rekindled and burning brightly. So she gathered all her strength and resolve to succeed, and moved forward from her hiding place at the base of the bush in the thicket to help her mysterious friend in any way she could, at any cost.

THE WARLORD AND his men all stared in horror and began to shake and tremble with cold fear. They couldn't believe what their eyes were seeing. It was impossible and yet, here it was between them and their small quarry. The warlord was more convinced than ever. Somehow the little witch had conjured this beast to come to her aid just when he had her at his mercy. First the stag and now this, whatever it was.

At that moment Pinofita opened his mouth and roared his battle cry. The warlord nearly dropped his sword, for the sound that came out of the huge brown beast with the red burning eyes was an ear-splitting squeak!

His mind raced, the witch had been in the tent the night this creature had first appeared in a fight with his dogs, and now the little witch was in the thicket, and this same beast had emerged from the thicket. The question that exploded in his head was, 'Is this creature and the little witch one and the same thing?'

So taken aback was he with that thought that he didn't react when Pinofita launched his first attack. The massive mouse leapt high and crashed down on the three men in the middle of the semi-circle. Weapons and men were thrown about like leaves in an autumn wind. Then Pinofita whipped his long tail around and sent another man sideways into the thicket. His eyes were burning bright in the morning sun and he faced the warlord who hadn't moved an inch.

Pinofita didn't notice the fifth hooded man behind him. The hunter had rolled away to avoid the first attack, drop to one knee and with shaking hands put an arrow to his bow. Drawing the bowstring back he took aim at the back of Pinofita's neck.

Just as the hooded man pulled the bowstring back to its fullest extent there was a dull thud. The hooded man slumped forward onto the cold ground, dazed from a blow to his head and changing the angle of the bow as he fell. The fingers released the bowstring and the arrow shot high, missed Pinofita but sailed right through the red swirling mist of the evil spirit. The evil one didn't bother to move and was totally unaffected by the arrow passing unimpeded though its red mist form, to land with a clatter in the rocks on the other side of the clearing.

HOLLY, HER FACE streaked with mud and blood, stood behind the hooded man who would have put an arrow into her beloved Pinofita, but was now outstretched on the ground. She had a grim look on her face and a small rock in her hand.

Hearing the thud behind him, Pinofita turned, and, in an instant, saw what Holly had done. He owed her his life he thought, and now he wasn't going to risk hers any longer. Pinofita's concern wasn't the warlord, it was the red swirling mist hovering above, he could sense evil in the red mist. As he looked at the evil one, his concern became panic, as he saw it open the mist, as it would a cloak, and reveal a red pulsing mass that its long bony fingers were reaching for.

Without any further thought Pinofita turned and in one huge bound landed next to Holly. She looked into his ruby red eyes still not quite believing her soft, little furry friend was now this huge fighting beast in front of her. However, when Pinofita spoke she knew without doubt it was her friend.

'Quick Holly,' he panted, 'Up on my back, we have to go, now, this very moment!' Without a second's hesitation, Holly reached up and grabbed his thick brown coat with two hands, and then threw a leg over his back and, gripping tightly with her knees as well as her hands, she shouted, 'I'm on, go, run as fast as you can. GO!'

The warlord rallied his men and as they stooped to pick up their weapons, one of them stopped and just stared at his spear lying on the ground. He pointed to it and, in a gruff but triumphant voice, called out, 'I got it, whatever it was, I got it!'

Every pair of eyes looked down at his spear. It was

lying on the ground where it had fallen when Pinofita had jumped onto the men in his first attack. It had a dark wooden shaft and a sharp metal blade, in fact it looked perfectly normal, except the sharp blade was covered in fresh, red blood … Pinofita's blood!

The warlord called triumphantly to his men and suggested they rubbed their hands in the blood on the spear, as a sign of their victory in injuring the brown beast of the thicket. The hooded men did as he suggested and felt it was a sign of victory, a victory they would complete in a short time from now.

One thing the hunters hadn't considered, was that blood has a scent that some animals could smell from a long way away, and blood usually meant that, whoever smelt of it, was injured and being injured, made them easy prey!

47

FLIGHT THROUGH THE FOREST

ERYK HELD BODA'S hand as they walked across the grassy area that led from their cottage to the forest. The news in the night from Edmund had really helped to raise their hopes that she would return soon but, as the day dragged on and there was still no sign of Holly, their hopes were beginning to fade.

'Isn't there something we can do to help?' pleaded Boda, looking up at her husband.

Eryk looked sympathetically at his wife.

'If I could think of something that would help, of course we would do it, but I can't. I don't know where she is. All we can do is hope she is safe and will return as soon as she can.'

'Hope,' said Boda wistfully, 'Is that all we have?'

'Sometimes,' said Eryk, 'It's all we have, and sometimes it's all we need, but we also have to believe in whatever hope we hold out for Holly.'

Still clutching the small sprig of holly with the two berries on it, Boda carried on walking with Eryk. So grief stricken was she, that no matter how many times Boda looked at the holly sprig to remind herself of her daughter, she'd never noticed the one sign that should have given her real hope. The reassuring sign had been in her hand since she first discovered Holly and Pinofita had gone into the forest. Despite having been plucked from the holly bush several days before, the two red berries, which by now should have shrivelled and dried, were still shiny red and full of life!

PINOFITA MADE GOOD progress running away from the warlord, the hunters and the troubling evil red thing he didn't understand, but he did understand it was to be avoided at all costs.

For Holly, riding on Pinofita was nothing like riding the huge grey wolf or the massive stag. His shape was different from theirs, particularly his body which became wider and wider the further you moved back from his shoulders. This made it difficult to grip with her legs and Holly continually slid forward and then had to push herself back with her hands gripping his thick coat.

As the warlord and his men kept up their chase, the evil one continued to hover above the warlord, but she was now beginning to realise where the source of the power that seemed to be helping the child was coming from. If she had been asked that question, she would have said, 'the power of the earth, water and sky.'

The realisation made her paler and a little bit smaller and, for the first time, she began to doubt her powers. Still, all she needed was to be in front of the child and to cast her last killing spell then she would be free.

The chasing group of men were not quite as fast as they had been that morning. Legs were tired, they were hungry and the huge beast that had come out of the thicket was something they didn't want to have to fight again anytime soon. The warlord did all he could to motivate and encourage them as they ran through the forest. The only thing that made it possible to continue the chase was that one of the men had finally retrieved the one remaining hound.

Despite his magical strength, after many hours of running Pinofita was now struggling as the pain in his left side had been growing and now was really hurting, hurting so much he knew he had to stop, which he did. Holly was glad of the chance to jump down from her awkward riding position since her arms and legs ached so much from having to grip and hang on.

As she dismounted, she said a heartfelt thank you to her still massive friend and patted his left side. Pinofita seemed to wince in pain and then Holly screamed with fright! She was staring at the hand she had just patted Pinofita with and was crying out in horror as she now realised what it meant. Her hand was red with blood, Pinofita's blood – he was badly injured!

48

THE SCENT OF BLOOD

HOLLY STOPPED SCREAMING but, with tears streaming down her cheeks, she put her arms around Pinofita's neck, and hugged him to her.

'Don't die, please don't die,' she wept.

'I won't,' said the familiar voice, 'but we have to think carefully what we do next. I am hurt but we have to keep going as they will still be following us.'

As Holly continued to hug her friend, he began to relax, to forget about the danger Holly had been in and, as he relaxed, he became calmer, the anger disappeared, and he began to get smaller. Holly slowly sank to the forest floor to lower herself to compensate for Pinofita's shrinking size until the wounded mouse was his normal size, cupped in her hand as she knelt on the forest floor.

'You rest now,' whispered Holly, 'I've had a good rest whilst you carried me. Now it's my turn to carry you.' With that, she stood and still cupping Pinofita in both hands, she ran as quickly and as carefully as she could in the direction she thought she had to go. Trusting her senses, Holly set off between the trees but, unbeknown to her, the direction she was now following was not the one she had been following before, that would have led to her home. This was different – but, for some reason, it was the way she sensed she had to go.

Progress was slow for Holly and, although she couldn't hear the men following her, every sense in her body told her they were still out there, somewhere behind her but she could also feel they were getting closer. She couldn't outrun them so she thought as she hurried along how she might outwit them.

THE CHASING GROUP gripped their weapons and ran as fast as they could and, with the dog still leading them, they followed Holly's scent trail through the trees, until they came to a shallow stream where the trail ended.

Holly hadn't hesitated when she saw the stream. She stepped straight in it and shuddered with the rush of cold water hitting her legs through her boots and trousers. It wasn't too deep, but she hoped it would make it difficult for the following men to know which way she had gone.

Carefully she walked with the current of the stream and kept going for a long time. Then she stepped out of the water and ran a few yards to the base of an old tree. Holly then carefully retraced her wet steps back to the stream and carried on in the direction the clear water was flowing. Maybe that would give her a bit more time before they caught up with her, at least that was what she hoped.

It wasn't long after Holly had entered the water that the warlord and his following group came to the stream's edge. The dog was confused since the scent it had been following now simply didn't exist, the water had swept it away.

The warlord tried not to show his anger. Instead, he ordered his men to take the dog and follow the stream. 'This is her easiest route, so that's the way the girl-witch will have gone. At some point she'll get out of the water and the dog will pick up her scent again. When that happens one of you come back for me and I'll rejoin you.'

Without questioning why their master would not be joining them, the hunters and the dog set off following the stream. When they were out of sight, the warlord turned to the evil spirit and called her to come closer.

Slowly the red evil spirit floated down to be closer to the warlord. She stopped and a strange silence grew between them.

'So now we are alone, tell me, why are you now so much paler than at first and smaller?' hissed the warlord into the evil one's dark faceless recess.

The evil one didn't answer for a few moments but did

realise she couldn't hide the truth from the warlord any longer.

The cracked and hollow voice broke the silence. 'I used most of my power to create the killing storm and—'

'Which hasn't killed anything or anyone yet!' snarled the warlord.

'—having used most of my power to create that storm, every time the girl evaded its power, it lost some of its force, and I could feel that too, so reducing my remaining power further, which shows in my size and colour.'

'So do you still have some power to complete my wish?' he growled.

Without saying a word, the evil spirit opened her swirling mist form and revealed the small pulsing red mass within.

'Just make sure you have the power to do what I wish for when the time comes, as it will soon.' With that the warlord turned to walk away.

Sensing the conversation was over, the red spirit again slowly rose and looked at the darkening evening sky, and to where part of her was still searching the forest for its small target.

The men had reached the spot where Holly had come out of the stream and walked to the tree. The dog bayed its excitement at finding the scent and rushed along the scent trail, with the hooded hunters with the blood red hands following. At the base of the tree, the hound stopped and just looked up into the branches. Again, the scent had ended, and the last trace of it was up against the trunk, so that was where it looked and howled.

'Aw, she's gone up the tree,' one of the men said.

'Can you climb?' said another.

'Well I'm not doing it,' said a chorus of voices.

No one wanted to climb up into the tree. The simple reason was that they didn't know what horrors awaited up there.

However, the horror that they then heard froze their blood and rooted them to the spot. Through the evening dusk that now shrouded the trees came the chilling call of a wolf, to be answered by the howling cries of other wolves. The darkening forest rang with the song of the hunting wolf pack closing in on the scent of blood!

The dog tore itself free from the handler that held it and ran off through the trees as fast as its four legs could take it. The hunters forgot all about loyalty to their master, and did the same, but they were much slower. The sixteen wolves that followed the men through the trees were faster and, as the evening darkened even more, their amber eyes burned with revenge and hunger.

'Wolves!' cried the warlord in alarm, as he heard the hunting cries of the one animal he feared more than any other in the forest. 'Why are they in this part of the forest? They live much further north. They shouldn't be anywhere near here.'

He drew his sword to give himself a bit more courage and then demanded of the evil one. 'Which way did she go? Where do we go now to find and finish her?'

The evil spirit didn't reply but did rise further into the evening sky and looked for the part of itself that still pulsed within the red storm. After several minutes, the evil spirit floated down to face the warlord, who was looking frantically around at the surrounding trees, still with his sword in his hand, his shaking hand.

'The storm is moving in a steady westerly direction, so it seems to know where the child is. Follow me; I will lead you.'

For the first time, the red spirit led the warlord, they went across the stream and then through the trees, the warlord having to run quickly to keep up with the swirling mass floating in front of him.

HOLLY WAS STUMBLING along now, nearly totally exhausted, her running made more difficult because she still held the wounded Pinofita in her cupped hands. He had reassured her he would be fine, he just needed to rest a bit longer. Holly was desperately worried about him. He had done so much for her, now she had to do everything she could for him.

The warlord was also desperately tired and worried. Worried about his men, for they hadn't answered his many calls to join him. The one good thing was that he hadn't heard the wolves howling again. But it wasn't a good thing for him, and it certainly wasn't a good thing for his men, since hunting wolves don't howl when they are eating!

49

A LAST DASH

THE WARLORD CONCENTRATED on the path ahead that the red evil spirit was taking. It was easy for the evil one. She didn't have to watch out for tree roots and big stones, whereas he did, and, for the ninth time after leaving the stream, he stumbled over yet another tree root and nearly fell headlong onto the forest floor.

Up ahead of the evil spirit and the warlord, Holly was now barely able to walk as she moved very slowly through the trees so tired was she. It was this slow pace that had allowed the red storm to find her again and now it began to move ever closer. In the end, she looked for a place where she and Pinofita could hide, and hopefully rest for a short while.

'I'm just going to rest for a bit Pinofita but first we need – I need – to find a safe place for us to hide.'

The small voice from her cupped hands replied, 'Take care Holly. They are probably closer than you think and listen out for the dog. Its barking will be the first noise you'll hear as they approach.'

'Just a minute,' whispered a breathless Holly, 'I'm going to sit in these bushes for a minute. The trees won't give me as much cover as these thick bushes will.'

With that Holly sat in the leafy branches of the bush and opened her cupped hands to place her little friend on her cape, now draped over her outstretched legs.

'Hello, my precious one,' she said tiredly, and smiled at her furry friend, who tried vainly to sit up, but then just groaned and fell back onto his side but continued looking up at her.

'I'm sorry if it was a jolty sort of ride in my hands, but you couldn't have clung on in my cape as usual, not with your side being hurt.'

'It was fine, better than being left out on my own in the woods,' he replied.

'It's getting darker now. Evening is really setting in, so I'm not sure about continuing in the dark. I don't think I know which part of the woods we are in. We've come such a long way.'

Pinofita looked up and said, 'Which way do you sense you need to go?'

'Oh, let me see, probably, oh probably that way.' Holly pointed over her shoulder through to the other side of the bush.

Pinofita suddenly jumped up with a painful squeak, and made a grab for Holly's nose, causing her to shriek and quickly move her head back out of the way of her friend's body and, in doing so lost her balance and toppled backwards into the bush. As Holly and Pinofita fell backwards the bush exploded with a shower of red fire and sparks, just where her head had been!

The spell hurled at her by the evil spirit had just missed hitting its target because of the quick action by her loyal friend, who had seen the streak of red light coming at them very quickly from the darkness of the trees opposite.

'Arrrrh,' shrieked Holly, realising what had just happened, and how close the spell had come to finding its target – her!

She quickly gathered Pinofita up in one hand and scrambled with a newfound energy, pushed her way through the side of the bush, and then through another one, then, once free of the bushes, she ran headlong through the trees. She didn't care which direction she took, all Holly wanted to do was to put as much distance between her and the following evil beings chasing them, and protect her wounded, furry friend.

With the last of her ebbing strength, Holly ran stumbling between the tree trunks and through the bracken. Her running was made all the more difficult by the dim evening light that seemed to fade with every step she took. Quick glances over her shoulder confirmed her worst worry, her tormentors were closing the gap between them and getting closer all the time. She could also feel the temperature dropping, which meant the red storm was getting closer. Holly pushed her way through some low scrub bushes, instead of trying to find a way around them and, seeing a space open up in front of her, she ran through the long grasses through the gathering cold and into a clearing where the snow was beginning to fall again. Above, the moon lit night sky was once again tinged red with the approaching storm.

It was a nightmare, but not one she was dreaming, it was real. The warlord's voice was getting louder, which distracted her, and then she lost her footing, stumbled and fell forward as the ground in front of her dropped away. Clutching Pinofita to her chest to protect him, Holly rolled head over heels several times and then crashed into something very hard, a steep rock face that rose up from the grass in front of her.

The impact knocked the breath out of Holly and so she sat, slightly dazed on the grass, with Pinofita lying sideways on her cloak that covered her legs. He was still breathing but his eyes were closed, and the only movement was the twitching of his whiskers. With no strength to get up and carry on, Holly watched, horrified, as the warlord and the red evil spirit came through the bracken and slowly descended the slope to stand in front of her, just a few yards away.

The triumphant, gloating look on the warlord's face made the dark veining even darker, and the glint in his dark eyes made Holly's blood run cold. To make matters even worse, the evil spirit floated in the chill night air just behind the warlord's left shoulder, waiting for the command to complete the warlord's wish.

Holly felt powerless to save Pinofita or herself. It was as if she was rooted to the ground in front and slightly to the side of the cold rock face. All she could do was to stare defiantly back at the warlord and wait for whatever fate was in store for her and her wounded, furry friend.

50

TO THE DEATH

HOLLY DIDN'T HAVE long to wait.

'Complete my wish and earn your freedom, finish her!' yelled the warlord staring with hate-filled eyes at Holly. Pinofita heard those horrible threatening words and even in his wounded state he felt his anger begin to rise again.

Without saying anything, the evil red spirit, with its two bony hands, parted the swirling pale red mist to reveal the remaining small portion of red pulsing matter.

Long talon-tipped fingers seized the red mass and began to fashion it into a pulsing red spear. Holly stared in horror at the fingers making the spear, transfixed to the spot, just waiting for the inevitable to happen. Her eyes were wide with disbelief as she watched the evil one complete the red spear and then, with the spear firmly held in its hand, it drew its arm back, high behind its pale swirling body.

No words passed Holly's lips. She just sat and stared in defiance at the warlord and the evil spirit, waiting for the arm to shoot forward and launch the spear at her and Pinofita.

Then her world changed forever.

With a blurring movement of its arm, the red evil spirit hurled the killing spear spell at Holly, who still didn't move. She just held her breath and felt tears form in her eyes as images of her parents, her home and happier times flashed through her mind.

In the red tinged moonlight, a shadow passed in front of Holly's eyes, the moon-lit shadow of Pinofita desperately making his last sacrifice to save his beloved friend and, in doing so, fulfilling the promise he had made to her when they had first set out on their adventure.

Pinofita grew with his growing anger and desperation to save Holly and was nearly cat size as he leapt up between Holly and the red spear spell. In a shower of red sparks the spell hit him full on the side. Uttering a pained squeak, he fell at Holly's feet, a large red wound on one side of his body. As Pinofita lay crumpled on the ground, his eyes desperately searched for Holly's as she came out of her trance with a jolt of cold realisation. She screamed in horror at what she saw as she quickly moved to kneel over her beloved friend. Their eyes met and, to Holly's despair, the bright black eyes began to dull in the brown, furry and bloodied body.

Then from the recesses of her mind came the awful memory of Pinofita saying to her. 'I would do anything for you, I'd even gladly give my life for yours.'

Holly reached out with her hand and her trembling fingertips gently touched the little brown body in front of her, hoping to offer some comfort to her brave friend. With angry and desolate tears in her eyes, she looked up at the warlord and the very pale evil spirit, not caring what happened to her now.

'You've failed again, can't you ever get anything right and rid me of that child?!'

The sound of the warlord's angry voice shattered the stillness of the red-tinged night and brought Holly out of her paralysing despair. She reached down to pull her cape off her legs so she could rise and run at her tormentors in a last desperate attempt to somehow defeat them. But her fingers came to rest on something hard. It was the tube with the shimmering powder in it. Quickly she reached into her pocket to retrieve it but, as she pulled it out of her pocket, a rough hand grabbed her wrist.

'No you don't not again, no magic spells, this time you'll suffer the fate you deserve.'

The warlord had seen Holly reaching into her pocket so had leapt forward to stop her doing whatever it was she was going to do.

'No more stags and not another huge mouse, not this time,' he snarled into her face and, with that, he wrenched the tube out of her hand and threw it over her shoulder. The crystal container shattered on the rock face.

Holly gasped at the sound of the breaking material, and her world crumbled, now she had no way of saving her friend; no way of defeating the warlord or this pale red swirling thing; or even of saving herself. Whilst staring with her eyes burning with hate and defiance at the warlord, what Holly didn't see was that the golden shimmering powder, now released from the broken tube was quickly sinking through the rock face and into the dark earth beyond.

The warlord looked over his shoulder at the evil one that was now a shrivelled version of what it had been, and only just hovering above the ground. It was like it had lost its power, other than the power that still resided in the red storm that was gathering in strength around them. He decided the evil spirit was of no further use.

'Right, I'll finish it myself then, since you can't,' he yelled at the evil one. The pale spirit made no response.

With his mind made up, the warlord fixed his evil stare on Holly and a grotesque grin of victory appeared on his dark face. Slowly, so as to savour the moment, he reached across his body with his gnarled, dark veined hand and gripped the hilt of his sword.

Slowly he drew his sword with his dark cruel eyes still fixed on Holly, who was kneeling next to the small, still form of Pinofita. He raised the weapon slowly above his head, and then let his other hand rise to form a double handed grip on the sword in readiness to deliver the final blow. The warlord had decided the only fate suitable for this little witch was to finish her the way he should have done to the old hag witch so many years ago, he was going to behead her!

With his arms fully raised and drawn back over his head, the warlord was ready to bring the sharp sword down in one last terrible cutting blow. A split second before he made that final downward killing sweep, his eyes were drawn to the rock face behind where Holly knelt. He couldn't understand why his attention was now so focused on the dark rock, instead of his helpless victim kneeling on the ground before him. Then, with increasing unease, he stared as a section of the rock seemed to melt and begin to reform into something else.

As he watched, in the rocky wall a pair of impossibly large eyes were forming, impossibly large green eyes that blazed with an intense fury. A fury that was directed at him. Fear, like a stream of freezing water, ran through his whole body.

He froze, unable to understand what he could now clearly see, in fact, he could hardly breathe. Then the face, wreathed in a mask of black, formed more fully around the furious green eyes.

When the huge face was fully formed, from behind it a shimmering light seemed to shine through the facial features. A light that seemed to come from behind the rocky wall, from within the dark earth itself and whatever else was behind the wall of ancient rock.

From her kneeling position Holly, who had been expecting the worst, was taken completely by surprise, first by the warlord seeming to freeze with his sword held high over his head, and secondly, by the beam of shimmering light. A shimmering light that warmed her and allowed a small spark of hope to flare again, sending tingles through her body.

Within seconds, the furious face in the rocks was replaced by an intense shimmering blue-white beam of light. In fact, not just a beam but a blazing tunnel of light that held the warlord and the evil spirit immobile in its grip.

They were trapped unable to move!

At first nothing else happened. Then, out of the light, a large bare-chested warrior appeared. His long hair and plaited beard framed his stern face and the war paint markings on his body declared him to be a chief from many years ago.

He held a sword in his right hand and his left fist was clenched and raised, as if calling for men to follow him. They did, a small group of proud ancient warriors came down the tunnel of light after their chief, their bodies ethereal and semi-transparent in the light.

Even though they couldn't move, the warlord and the evil spirit screamed in fear and panic as the band of warriors approached them. Despite all their efforts to move, they couldn't, the light held them fast.

From her kneeling position on the ground next to the prone body of Pinofita, just on the edge of the tunnel of light, Holly watched in complete amazement and disbelief.

The tall leader of the ghostly warriors walked up to the warlord and, with his sword, knocked the warlord's blade out of his grip. Again the warlord screamed his terror. The ghostly warriors then seized both the warlord and the evil spirit, picked them up and held them high above their heads. Then the group turned and, with their captives weakly struggling in their grip, they marched back down the tunnel of light. Realising what was happening, the warlord and the evil spirit screamed with fear, but their cries were soon lost as they, and the warriors that carried them, disappeared down the tunnel of light, through where the rock face stood and into the dark earth beyond.

Holly blinked her eyes in disbelief and, from where she sat, she just looked on at the amazing events. As the warriors and the captives they carried disappeared down the tunnel of light, it began to dim. The chief came to stand before Holly and looking down on her, his stern face changed, and he smiled. Her tear, mud and blood-stained face looked up at him, her world shattered and broken, since her small, furry friend lay motionless and bleeding in the grass in front of her.

The warrior chief then knelt on one knee and raised his left arm over Pinofita's inert body. His fist was still clenched but, when he opened it, grains of shimmering golden powder fell onto the tiny body. He stood, bowed to Holly and then he too walked back down the fading tunnel of light. As the light finally disappeared, the rock face could be seen again, lit by the pale red moonlight.

After the beam of light disappeared, something else remarkable happened, the forest night sky changed. The red storm that had been slowly approaching where Holly was kneeling, began to shudder and shrink. It continued to shrink and then finally swirled into a fireball, a fireball that fell from the sky and returned to the exact point from which it was launched.

In an explosion of red sparks and flames, the fireball landed on the wooden tower of the castle setting it ablaze. So intense was the heat that not only did all the wood burn, but the stones too became so hot they eventually crumbled and turned to dust. When the next autumn storms blew, the dust would be blown away throughout the forest, so leaving no trace whatsoever of the castle that once stood in the huge blackened clearing. A clearing that would slowly, over time, become green woodlands once again and a home for the forest creatures that had once lived there.

With the destruction of the red storm, a full white moon appeared in the velvety summer night sky, flooding the clearing with a ghostly pale light.

With hope surging through her whole body, Holly eagerly watched the shimmering grains sink into Pinofita's body. After a few moments, and to her complete dismay, no small dot of light appeared within his body. She closed her eyes and, with tears of burning sadness streaming down her mud and blood-stained cheeks, she lifted her head and cried her misery out loud to the night sky in her grief.

As she lifted her face skywards, behind her, the green-eyed face reappeared in the rock wall and with a gentle smile the pursed lips blew a soft breath towards Pinofita. A bit like you would if you blew on the embers of a fire to encourage the flames to rise again.

His fur ruffled in the soft breath and then a tiny dot of light appeared in the small body, a light that glowed with an intense brightness and then grew and grew and grew!

Light filled the clearing, so intense it even blotted out the moonlight causing Holly to close her eyes, catch her breath and to hold it until the light subsided. Hope soared throughout her entire body. But, before she could open her tightly shut eyes, a small whiskery nose pushed into her hands and a familiar little voice said, 'Hello Holly, are you all right?'

Her tears of misery changed to tears of joy that shook Holly's whole body as she carefully cradled her furry friend once more in her shaking hands and raised him up so she could repeatedly gently kiss his head.

They sat together huddled under the rock face, talking about what had happened when they had been separated. How Holly now understood about Pinofita's magical powers. Sometimes they just sat in happy silence, until the morning sun crept over the tops of the surrounding forest trees and the dawn chorus filled the morning air.

51

HOPE

IN HER VILLAGE, Holly's parents woke to a bright sunny day, a lovely blue summer sky complete with fluffy clouds and warm sunshine. They couldn't believe it, the red storm had finally gone, no longer was the sky tinged with that hateful red colour. In simple terms, it all looked peaceful and wonderfully normal again.

As they stood at their bedroom window looking up at the swifts in the sky, Boda turned to Eryk, her eyes filled with a shining glint of hope. 'It's all normal, as it should be, do you think that means …?'

'I think it does,' he said in a slightly trembling voice.

'Edmund was right about the legend of the green wolf rider being true, wasn't he? I find that so hard to believe, but it must be true, mustn't it?' Boda continued.

'Yes,' agreed Eryk, 'The green figure did rise up to save the forest, and us. Hopefully now things are back to normal, for good.'

'But she's done it as well, Holly has done whatever she needed to do to get rid of the storm surely?' protested Boda.

'Of course she has,' chuckled Eryk, 'Our brave little Holly and her even smaller, furry friend, they've played their part, I'm sure of it!'

After a hasty but happy breakfast Boda and Eryk went into the village to share their happiness with all the other villagers. As they went outside, they saw the village coming to life again, people laughing and going about their everyday jobs. They went to Edmund's house where they hugged him again for the exciting news he had brought to the village. All would finally be well for them once they had their daughter and her special little friend safely back home.

They returned to their cottage and walked into the garden to sit on the rough wooden bench to wait for the happy reunion they felt must happen sometime very soon. Boda still clutched the sprig of holly with the two bright red berries, as she had done since she first found it on the table within the hastily drawn heart. Eryk looked at his smiling and happy wife, now truly happy for the first time in a long time.

HOLLY, WITH PINOFITA in his usual place by her neck in her hood, stood and looked around where they were and, in doing so came face to face with a deer standing feeding in the meadow flowers on the slope of the mound to the side of the rock face. She smiled because the deer didn't run away, it just moved slowly further up the grassy slope totally unafraid. As she looked at her surroundings it slowly came back to her, this was it, the clearing, the grassy meadow and the strange shaped mound with the rock face at one end. This was where she had first created Pinofita.

Then her mother's after-supper tale of the legend about the special burial place in the forest for those good, brave ancient warriors came racing back out of her memory. The strange ghostly warriors that came out of the tunnel of light, who had taken the warlord and the evil one, must have come from inside this mound. So it must be a barrow that her mother talked about, a very, very special barrow!

Holly, with Pinofita looking out from under her hood, climbed onto the top of the barrow. Then she slowly turned to look at the clearing where so many things had started and had now ended. She knelt and placed both hands on the earth, her fingers gently entwined within the grass and flower stems. She felt strange and different but she also felt happier and stronger than at any other time in her life. With her eyes shut she thanked the figure with the green eyes and smiling face for her pet Pinofita, the friendship of the grey wolf, her rescuer the huge stag and then the ancient warriors for their help and kindness and promised to visit them again. If she had kept her eyes open at that moment, she might have seen the kind green-eyed face that beamed at her from within the nearby flowers.

Having stood and made sure Pinofita was safely in his usual place snuggled by her neck in her hood, Holly checked the angle of the sun and walked towards the tree line to the south of the clearing. She thought she could remember the way home she had found before. At least, that's what she hoped!

POSTSCRIPT

A NEW BOND FORMS

A PAIR OF BRIGHT amber eyes watched undetected from the cover of the trees as Holly and Pinofita were happily reunited once more with their family.

The wolf's gaze was one of friendship and a growing respect and fondness for the brave girl in the green cape and her magical little furry companion.

With the comforting knowledge of where Holly lived, and feeling the hand that had rested lightly on his head lift – the hand that had urged him to follow the two adventurers – the watcher silently turned and began his long journey back to the high forest, confident he would meet them again.

START YOUR OWN
ADVENTURE
WITH NATURE

Keep a record of how you have helped nature

Date	How I helped nature

You might save a bee from a puddle. Or help a snail cross the road. Or plant a tree and watch it grow ...

Make your own Pinofita

Hint ... use whichever materials you have; they do not need to be what Holly used.

Look for faces in nature (human,
animal and supernatural)

... then have a go at drawing them.

Finally ...

The scientific name for trees commonly known as
pine trees and conifers is:

Pinophyta
(pronounced pea-nof-i-ta)

... so now you know the secret of Pinofita's name!

ACKNOWLEDGEMENTS

MY HEARTFELT THANKS go to five very special people who have shared the story as it developed, and in their specific ways have helped make the final version what it is.

Firstly, to my wife Linda for her patience during all the hours I spent shut away in the morning room writing the story on my computer and creating the illustrations, and her wonderful contribution of proofreading the text and making grammatical corrections.

Secondly, to my good friend Jill Whiting who read an early transcript and made some very pertinent suggestions, which have now been incorporated into the final version.

Thirdly, to nine year old Jemima Knight, my first target age group reader, who provided the necessary motivation and encouragement to keep going with her very positive feedback.

Fourthly, to Lorna Brookes, my editor at Crumps Barn Studio, for her creative suggestions and artistic book cover, as well as her belief in me and the original story.

Finally, to Octavia (the owner of Octavia's Bookshop, an award-winning local bookshop), who read the final manuscript and provided wonderful advice on both the story and key next steps, as well as the very encouraging first sentence of her review ... *"All in all, it is a well written, atmospheric, gripping adventure story."*